LONELY BOY BLUES

Alan Kapelner

Tough Poets Press
Arlington, Massachusetts

ISBN 978-0-578-46786-3

This edition published in 2019 by
Tough Poets Press
49 Churchill Avenue, Floor 2
Arlington, Massachusetts 02476
U.S.A.

www.toughpoets.com

To my brother, Nat, who fought bravely for the stuff that freedom is made of.

CHAPTER 1

WALKING WITH yourself in the land of the sky blue people and hating yourself for the ache that pumps and pumps in your lonely flesh is not my idea of a good time.

Now let's get this straight:

The flesh spins to the skull, and discharging in the skull lives the brain, jackpot brain, passport to a future, mardi-gras destiny drowning in confetti and wine. The future belongs to you, you are the future. Very elementary, my dear brain. Paste yourself to the bandwagon. Be the spoke in its wheel, you bitter American Dream brain, brain most likely not to succeed as a spoke, brain not knowing where it's going, but it's going. Oh, it's a good brain as far as good brains go, but as far as good brains go it went. There's one in every household.

Yes, passport to a future, the future of a jar! Rare, exquisite specimen! Stunning contribution to science! A brain by any other name stinks! Very elementary!

Oh, psychiatrists of the world, parade this brain before the population, you have nothing to lose but your Freuds!

Well, start the day with a smile. The day is so clear you can see a bum bum a dime on Columbus Circle. And today is Thursday. And it's in the morning. And on this Thursday morning of Our Lord and My Life I will benefit society by parking in front of the Rialto Theatre. I light a cigaret. Observe the grace of the flame and the hole in my pants.

Female models for the Beef Trust pass me and don't notice me, and down with them if they don't notice me, says I, the bored young man of Times Square. I narrow my bloodshot eyes and blow smoke in their lumpy faces, the smoke that satisfies.

My culture is pained by the cheesecake film at the Rialto, and so I give the front of Child's the distinction of my company.

Fifty-eight cents for a veal cutlet. Fifty-eight cents for a veal cutlet? I spit at their veal cutlets, tomato sauce and one vegetable. Don't spit in the street, son. Remember the Johnstown Flood! But, hell, my Pop spits at steaks. Steaks, he hates! Well, my Pop will never be accused of being a mental giant, since he thinks I'm the strong boy of the world. My Pop thinks he's right and if he thinks he's right let him think he's right and let it go at that. My Pop, right or wrong, my Pop.

How's my hair and dig my tie, and a terrible curse on that cockamamie, Emily Post and her goddamn Bible on Formal Introductions, for mine eyes have seen the glory of the coming of a tight sweater and a short skirt, and her face is so pale, and oh how red her lips are, and don't sell her long hair short!

Come to me, my paleface baby, cuddle up and don't be pale. I nod so nicely and she passes me so swiftly. That's a very cruel thing to do, Miss Red Lips. Can't you see that you're for me? Long is my truelove's hair! Short is my truelove's skirt!

Yes, today is Thursday, and it's in the morning, and the hunt, the luscious hunt is on! Picture yourself on the hunt in the morning, and don't be ashamed of yourself if you can't picture yourself. I am a guy with a remarkable constitution. I read Joyce's "Ulysses!"

Don't stop me if you've heard this before, but where oh where is that sweater taking that girl? I, so and so, hereby declare priority rights on that! I will make love to that and that will make love to me, and I will marry that. Then I will meet the parents of that, and that will say to them: introducing my husband . . . Boy meets that. Boy marries that. Get me Hollywood! Hello, is that you Zanuck?

Her parents will be proud of their new son. They will look me over and I will look them over, and they will know and I will know that their daughter discovered gold, and money will be collected to build her a monument for choosing me. That's a fact, and can you push around facts?

When a body meets a body coming through the rye. My girl's body, the body of the month. Priceless, handle with care. Silence, man at work. I will say: pardon me, but didn't I—no! My girl has class and will not fall for didn't I. I will say: you must remember me. That's it! The so very original line, feeble enough to creep alongside Old Ironsides! Then she will smile and I will smile and we will talk about the party where we never met, and I am laying odds right here and now that we will be the Act of God of our time. I met my wife on a Thursday morning!

You can run me, and, oh, sweet Christ, please don't walk me, to the nearest ungraded class if I try to pick her up in front of the Paramount when Charles Boyer is at the Paramount. Say I'm wrong and you're saying to hell with the opinion of American Womanhood. Inspect it this way: Boyer has a continental lingo and I was born in East St. Louis, and no cracks. My sister had a crush on the Darling of France that ran to 25c a week for photographs, and don't forget the enclosed postage. I said to her: wipe the drool from your lips. She said: Charles, you were meant for me and I was meant for you. . . . My sister was not very bright.

My girl snubs the French Thrill and ganders at dresses. She has an eye for the green dress. I don't go for green dresses, but is it a crime to wear a green dress, and if it's good enough for my girl isn't it good enough for you?

I can pull the act now. I can be smooth. I can say: a green dress fits your personality. And she will look up and say: really? And I will say: really. Profound dialogue! But no! I am strictly the you-must-remember-me type. She's passing up the green dress. That's copacetic with me, since I don't go for that, but if my girl wants it she gets it, and is it not the inalienable right of every American girl to wear any damn dress she pleases? Where the hell do you think you are—in Berlin?

Does she know I'm on the hunt? Is she saying: come on you, you with that stare in your 20-20 vision, pick me up, I'm your girl.

Yes, you are my girl, and I will whisper my name and how I hope your name is Kathleen. I will take you home, Kathleen, and you will take me home, Kathleen. Oh, darling, how much do I love you, I'll tell you no lies, how deep is the ocean, how high is the sky? Oh, look at me, your lover when the moon hangs low, your lover when there is no moon, and I'll knock you out in the rain or under the sun. I will take you home, Kathleen. You must remember me!

My girl stops at the Astor. The story of our romance begins at the Astor. Oh, the hunt and now the kill. When I grow old I will tell my grandchildren how I met their grandmother at the Astor. If you ask me, I can write a book.

Kathleen, you have made me happy. I was never really happy before. I sleep with two brothers in one bed. Can you be happy with three in a bed? But now life will be as fine as wine, cold in the summer, warm in the fall, hot in the winter and that ain't all! We will have a bed of our own, and a hunk of you and me will be born in this bed, and we will label her Sylvia. My mother's name is Sylvia, and what a portrait I have of how you will love my mother. I will say: Mamma, meet my wife!

Kathleen, dear wife, here I come! Here comes your husband, his heart on his face! You must remember your husband! You must remember your husband! Oh, dear wife!

But who the hell is this old man, this matinee idol of 1898 with the flush of good food in his face? What law gives him the right to hold you like that? Take your hand off my wife's ribs, the mother of my child! Kathleen, must you give him that toothpaste smile? Mister, where are you taking my wife? Kathleen, don't break your husband's heart! Mister, you're an old man with grey hair and the way you clutch my young wife makes me want to cry! Kathleen, observe my tears!

Say, can he be your father? How do you do, sir? I'm your daughter's husband, your son-in-law, born on the fourth of July. With your daughter by my side I'll be a text for Dale Carnegie. And, sir, if you are alone and in need of a home, why, just come home and live with us. The invitation is for life! You, me, Kathleen and Sylvia, your grandchild! And when I come home at night we will sit down and eat and after we eat we will smoke a cigar and after the cigar we will put Sylvia to bed and watch her fall asleep, and then I will build a fire and we will light up fresh cigars and discuss the news while Kathleen knits and reads the manufactured novels of Kathleen Norris. What I promise is no lie, sir! May I call you Poppa, sir? May I call you sir, Poppa? My hand is my bond, sir! Buy a bond, Poppa!

But, man to man, are you her father? Kathleen, is this lush your old man? Is this Civil War Vet the grandfather of our daughter? Kathleen, you must tell me these things. I'm by your side. I can touch your hand. I can touch his hand! I can smell your perfume. He smells, too! And that strange sound you hear is my groan. Please tell me, my wife, why does he hold you like that and why do you let him hold you like that? And where are the two of you going? Oh, God, they will not let me live these days!

Look how they walk to the desk, cheek to cheek, the pathological Romeo and the sex-starved Juliet. Look how the clerk smiles at the old man. I do not like that smile.

I die inch by inch while I see the clerk with the funny smile hand the old man a key, and I'm so dead, so dead when the old lips of the old man kiss my wife's lips that are oh so young, and I think of ruined men watching castles fall, and I say: for God's sake, Kathleen, don't enter that elevator with Mr. Methuselah! I know now he is not your father. Fathers do not kiss their daughters the way he kissed you . . . I went down to the St. James Infirmary, pronounced Hotel Astor, to see my baby there, she was stretched out on a long white table, so sweet, so cold, so bare.

Kathleen, Kathleen. Kathleen. The elevator shut in my face and I saw it go up. I saw the clerk with the funny smile whisper something to a bellhop with a funny smile, and I stumbled out of the hotel, crying and ashamed, alone and lonely. A drugstore on the corner had a sale on razor blades. I thought of my wrists.

Dear wife, you may read this story. You may remember me following you. You may remember Charles Boyer and the green dress and Mr. Methuselah. And you may remember the clerk with the funny smile. But, Kathleen, you do not know me, you do not know me. But I know you. You are my wife and I am your husband and we are the parents of Sylvia, and after you went and did it at the Astor I went home on that Thursday morning with a terrible sickness.

Oh, Kathleen, did you ever watch sugar in hot tea? It sinks quickly, melts quickly, dies quickly. I went to sleep that night with my two brothers, Joe and Skinny, in one bed, and the bed was hot, and I began to sink very quickly, melt very quickly, and Skinny saw me and asked why a misery was sticking out of my face, and I said: go to sleep, Skinny, go to sleep. And he said: can I sleep when a misery sticks out of your face? And I said, quote: I will tell you the truth, my little brother, I do not like what is going on in America. Unquote.

Oh, Kathleen, I am dying very quickly.

There will now be a two minute silence for my dead heart.

CHAPTER 2

SOMETIMES I would beg. A derelict roaming the streets, eyes in the gutter.

Sometimes I would yell. My voice would split the wall.

Sometimes my voice was so soft. A lover in a movie.

Sometimes I would shake Kathleen. A mouse in the mouth of a cat.

One night I hit her. Her body ran to the floor. A terrible moan twisted out of her lips. It stretched into hours. The clock said three hours. My Pop says I'm the strong boy of the world, prize package of the human race. I hit my wife again. And the terrible moan came again.

Then she said: yes. She finally said: yes. Yes, she would go away with me. We had a place in the country. We packed a few things. I brought along my knife.

We got there in the morning. It was hell that day. I waited and waited for the darkness. It was the longest day since the world began. Then the sun made place for the moon. The darkness came. The moon hid behind the clouds. The darkness became very black.

We finished supper. Kathleen knew how to cook. Things tasted good. Kathleen said she'd clean the pots. I read a paper. Kathleen cleaned the pots. I put the paper away. I brought out the knife. I released the blade. I saw my face in the shine of the steel. I looked like an animal.

I walked softly to Kathleen. She was bending over the sink. The water was running. Her back grew big, so big. She didn't hear me coming. I raced the blade into her back. I raced it again and I raced it again and again, and then I felt the blade cut through a tough bone. It was a very tough bone. I shut off the water.

Kathleen pitched to the floor, her body lazy and her face a mask of dumb pain. I saw her blood crawl through the slashes my blade made in her dress. It fascinated me. Then I kicked her ribs. I kicked her ribs seven times. Then I kicked her face. My toe ripped her nose. The blood stopped crawling.

I walked through the woods with a shovel and a searchlight. I walked up a hill. I started to dig. I stopped after awhile. The pit was roomy. The dirt was black and I saw worms. I lit a cigaret. I remembered that ad in the papers: EXPERIENCED GRAVEDIGGER WANTED AT ONCE. PROGRESSIVE FIRM. TOP-NOTCH SALARY. STEADY WORK. OVERTIME PAY. FRIENDLY CONDITIONS. APPLY AT FORT MADISON CEMETERY . . . Dear Sirs: I am a very experienced gravedigger.

I went back to the house. I picked up Kathleen. She was heavy. Her dress was stiff with the starch of dry blood. My fingers jammed into her wounds. I walked through the woods and up the hill. I threw Kathleen into the pit. I spit at her body and threw a rock at her. I shoveled the dirt back into the pit. I patted the dirt with the back of my shovel. I did a good job. The freshness of the dirt would die by morning. No one would know. I lit another cigaret.

I sat on her grave until I finished the cigaret. I thought of a baseball game I once saw, winning run on second, two out and a man next to me said he had heart trouble. Then I walked down the hill and through the woods and turned to the grave and spit at the night. The moon broke out of the clouds. The man in the moon had veins in his face.

I went back to the house. I finished the paper. I undressed and went to bed. I felt good and tired. The sleep was healthy.

I got up early in the morning and packed the few things we brought the day before. I walked out of the house and through the woods and up the hill. I looked at my wife's grave and the freshness of the dirt was dying. I walked down the hill and through the woods and over to the road and then a mile to the station. I took the train home.

A few days later I was standing in front of the Rialto Theatre with a friend of mine. We were talking about things and watching the girls pass. And out of the crowd came Kathleen, my wife, with her tight sweater, her short skirt, her pale face, her red lips and long hair.

She walked over to me. She was smiling. One of those funny smiles. An old man with grey hair passed and looked at my wife and my wife looked at him and the old man walked on toward the Astor, and my wife kept looking at him. I felt my pocket for my knife. It was there. My friend said he was going. I said: see you later.

I drew in hard on my cigaret. The smoke spit from my mouth. I thought of the woods and the hill and the pit and the dry blood and the worms in the black dirt. I took it easy. I tried to smile. She placed her hand on my hand. It was a warm hand. I flipped my cigaret into the gutter. A taxi ran over it.

She said: Hello.

I said: Hello.

She said: How are you?

I said: Okay, how are you?

She said: I feel swell.

I said: That's swell.

She said: And I feel hungry.

I said: Me, too.

She said: Let's eat.

I said: Good idea.

We went into Child's. We ordered veal cutlets, tomato sauce and one vegetable. The price was fifty-eight cents.

Someone screamed in the street. I opened my eyes. I looked at the clock. It was time to get up. The window was closed and the room was hot.

Skinny's legs were around my belly and Joe's face was smeared with one of those groggy looks.

I had to be at work in an hour.

I drew the shade.

I began to dress.

My socks were dirty.

CHAPTER 3

THE GREY fingers of a fog choked the streets, and Mabel poked a red stick across her lips and whispered dirty names at the early morning gloom. She completed the painting of her lips and stepped back to investigate her face and body through a mirror, and she felt glutted with satisfaction over the sensual lines of her dress that curved around the warm places of her torso. *In my sweet little Alice-blue-gown I will wander all over this town.*

Mabel dear, hurry. Breakfast is ready.

The call of the wild, the call of the wild mother. Hurry, dear Mabel. Hurry to your prune juice, roll and coffee. The Anderson Breakfast Special. Prices do not change after 10 A.M.

She entered the kitchen and Chesty's mouth was pregnant with the chunk of a roll. She looked at the clock and looked at her mother's sweaty scalp and sat down, gritted her teeth and bathed her throat with prune juice. *I thank thee, Lord, for my daily prune juice.*

She said: Just give me coffee, and no arguments.

Her mother said: But, Mabel, how can you start the day right with just coffee?

She said: Good God, must we go through this sermon every morning of my life?

Chesty said: The Daily Wail of Mabel Anderson, by Mabel Anderson.

She said: Isn't His Majesty late for work?

Chesty said: Now don't you permit your dyed redhead to worry about His Majesty.

She said: Oh, go and . . . catch a train!

Chesty said: Catch a train?

She said: I said catch a train!

Chesty said: But, Mabel, how can you catch trains?

She said: Mother, from what side of the family does my brilliant brother inherit his brilliance?

Her mother said: My father was a very wise man.

She said: Wise guy, grandson of mother's wise father.

Her mother said: Please don't fight. You'll wake up the boys, and, Chesty, you'd better hurry.

She said: Give my love to your defense plant.

Chesty said: Beware of the Johnson Motor Company bearing

machines.

He took a last swig of his coffee and said he wouldn't be home for dinner, since his body and soul had to appear at the Draft Board that night. He plucked his coat and hat from a hook, said goodbye and the stairs in the hall squeaked from the squeeze of his weight.

Grab your coat and grab your hat, leave your worry on the doorstep, just direct your feet to the G.I. side of the street.

Mabel sucked in her coffee and watched her mother's long fingers cleaning the sink, and she wondered from what side of the family did she inherit her own knotty fingers. It seemed to her that her mother's fingers were not in melody with her parched arms, and that her mother's relic of a body had no legitimate right to her fingers. It seemed to her that the long fingers were deliberately screwed to her wrists to insult her own malformation.

She said: Where's Pop?

Her mother said: He left at six.

The early bird catches the timeclock.

She said: How much money have you got?

Her mother said: I can only give you a quarter, darling.

She said: Well, holy hell, does Pop think there's a law against leaving me money? And how do you expect me to look for work on a quarter?

Her mother said: Then don't look, Mabel. Not today. You know how much I'd like you home with me. Just the two of us, darling.

She said: Well, wouldn't that be cozy! No, thanks. I'll look for work. Hand over that great big quarter!

And the condemned girl had eaten a hearty breakfast.

She walked to the bedroom, slipped into her coat and wondered why in the world won't that telegram come from Washington asking her to report for duty. Hadn't she applied at Civil Service two months ago? Hadn't she patriotically answered their national appeal for girls, girls, girls? Good God, the government is in one helluva fix! If this be treason make the most of it. She planted a blue flower in her hair.

Soft footsteps approaching forced her to forsake the sweet luxury of looking into the mirror. She turned to see her mother, and she felt herself swimming in the thick lava of idolatry that overflowed her catgreen eyes. Such was the constant state of affairs in her life, the constant play of lights and shadows streaking her canvas—and what to do about it? *Oh, Civil Service Commission, my fate is in your files.*

Her mother said: Darling, you will take care of yourself.

She said: Yes, darling, darling will take care of herself.

Her mother said: If any man looks at you, you will look away, won't you?

She said: Mother, I solemnly vow not to be raped today.

Her mother said: Oh, Mabel, Mabel is that nice?

She said: It's all according how you look at it, mother. Goodbye, and I'll see you anon, as they say in novels.

Her mother said: Are you forgetting to kiss mother?

She slid her red lips across the fibre of mother's pasty yellow face. *A tribal ritual copywritten by Mrs. Harry Anderson.*

She left the house, her ears battered with her mother's last warning on the men in the subways, the men in the streets and please, Mabel, steer clear of the crouching men in the cellars. *One bright and shining light that keeps me wrong from right is my mother's eyes—and voice!*

When she reached the low rung of the stairway she at once plunged for the mailbox. The mailbox was no prosaic square of tin to her, it was in spirit a deposit box for results, a current to wash away the cling of reality that reared its variety of heads in the cloisters she called her home. *Neither snow, nor rain, nor heat, nor gloom of night, thank God, stays these couriers from the swift completion of their appointed rounds to the mailbox of Mabel Anderson, thank God.*

A letter from Private Ty Fitzgerald was addressed to Miss

Mabel Anderson.

She crammed the letter into her bag and thought she'd read it in the standing room of the subway.

Ty Fitzgerald, she thought, wet, nervous hands, splotchy skin, hungry Irish eyes never smiling. She remembered her first kiss, negotiated by Ty, Mister Romance of the East and points West. It was at a party and the boys began to spin a bottle, and the girls blushed and protested much too much. She entered a dark room and Ty was there, and he held her where she was never held before, and he eased his tongue into her mouth and crazy sensations and snapping quivers made a mess of her flesh.

The aftermath was vivid to her. She had remained awake nights obsessed with the dampness of the kiss. She had a general idea that storks did not bring babies, and she wondered if the kiss contained the serum of production, and she rocked in her bed, and one night she rose from her bed, feverishly tore off her nightgown, stood naked and ashamed before her mirror and swore she saw a swell bubbling from her belly, and then the word *mother* piously sneaked through her lips, and she ran back to bed and cried salty tears over the abysmal fate of a thirteen year old girl in the throes of birth, and the black catastrophe of marriage to Ty Fitzgerald, age fifteen.

And then came the march of boys. Boys flying their boasting flags of experience, boys turning into men overnight. She recalled that young English dancer with the matured halitosis. One rainy afternoon he took her to a cheap hotel and they had spent hours in a dirty room, and she winced over the exotic thrills she did not receive in that dirty room with its bed of brown lice as crawling spectators.

Oh, there was Angelo and Marty, Irving O'Hara, Jack Sherman and Thomas Thomas, Jr., guys with quick lips spewing flip quips, myopics hellbent for frustration on the 4.15. And there was always the faithful and well-trained Ty, the warm dog whom she led here and led there and allowed him to kiss her here and kiss her there.

And then came the night of sheer boredom in a hallway when she thought of working crossword puzzles while Ty was going through the passionate paces of one of his special kisses. *46 down: 8 letter word for passport.* And after the kiss she patted Ty's head and told him to take a walk for himself, and he obediently took a walk for himself. And then came the news that he had enlisted in the Army, and she had received the queer pleasure of being an Army Recruiting Station in reverse. *Join the Army through the hallway of Mabel Anderson.*

All these boys, and her mother, too. She had manipulated each and every one of them as a visa to lessen her stay at home. She was able to instinctively detect the program of their actions and sexual diets, and she commanded the verve to upset their programs and constipate their diets. She twisted them and listed them, used them and bruised them.

One morning she had made a date with three boys on the same corner at the same time. She hid herself in a doorway and watched the three boys pace the street, look up the street and down the street, the three unknown to each other. And there she was, a prostrated victim of hilarity in the doorway, her eyes weeping laughter over their shifty eyes and wriggling feet. *Oh, what a beautiful morning, oh, what a beautiful day.*

One hour passed and they left the corner and she left the doorway, and a roadster pulled up to the curb and she was asked if she was going the driver's way, and she went his way. They rode out to a reservoir and the man parked his car and said he was married, but she was lovely, and he asked her for unconditional surrender, and she thought of the three boys on the same corner at the same time, and she laughed and said it was too bad, but she wasn't going in for married men that year, and that he should try her next year. The man chewed off part of his lip and told her to go to hell and walk back. *Millions for defense, but not one body for tribute.*

She didn't walk back. A milk truck brought her back to the city and back to hell where she had been told to go, home. *Oh, bury me not on the lone prairie, where the mothers howl and the wind is free.*

A train pulled into the station and Mabel and forty customers piled in. She read a newspaper over a man's shoulder. BATTLE RAGING IN EUROPE. She thought of Ty in uniform, Ty gripping a gun, and she tried very hard to think of Ty becoming a hero, and she gave up. She opened his letter and plowed through his crazy scrawl.

Mabel honey,

I sent you so many letters and why, why don't you answer them, honey? When they yell out mail I never get the answer I want to get, and I feel like dying in a hole. Please, honey, answer me and tell me what you're doing and how you are and you can leave out who you're seeing at night. Gee, you don't know how important you are to me.

The guys in the barrack gas about their girls and I rave about you and they produce pictures of their girls and I have no picture of you, and when I told them how beautiful you are, they didn't believe me, they didn't believe me. They always say produce or shut up. And I shut up.

Gee, honey, would you send me a picture of yourself? I remember that day we went swimming and how nifty you looked in your orange and white bathing suit, and don't think I don't remember how the wolves on the beach looked at you, and the girls looked, too. And you were with me, and, Christ, I was one proud guy. Will you send me a picture of you in your orange and white bathing suit and your red hair falling over your shoulders? I want to show these guys what I got and what you got. Will you, honey? Gee, I hope you will, honey.

Well, honey, the guy next to me is shining his shoes, and he says I better knockoff the letter because the lights around here go out at 10, so I must knockoff, and I get on my knees for you to answer me and send me a picture of you in your orange and white bathing suit. I'll show these guys!

Ty

P.S. I hide a piece of paper under my mattress. Every time I write you I make a note of the date. So far I put down nine dates, nine letters. When I reached six I said I'm not writing to her any more until she answers, but now it's number nine and I know I'd be a damn liar if I said I'd stop now until you answer. Guess I'll be putting lots more dates and numbers on that piece of paper I hide under my mattress even if you don't answer. I know I will. Guess it's because I love you so much. Guess it's that, all right. Guess so.

How to win Mabel and influence soldiers with orange and white bathing suits in nine easy letters.

The train stopped at Thirty-fourth Street, and Mabel saw a boy kiss a girl, and the girl said she'd meet him under Macy's clock that night, and the boy left the train with Mabel, and his eyes raced over her tendencies as they exited to the street. Mabel gave him one of her well-what-the-hell-are-you-looking-at looks, an optical weapon she had mastered in her street sessions with the male animals, and the boy sunk his head into his neck and lost himself. Mabel thought of the girl he left behind in the subway, a girl with watery eyes who should save her money to buy a stiletto and carve the solid scad of dirt from her lover's heart under Macy's clock.

She walked up the street, dictated by the pat routine she had obeyed for the past eight months: visit the department stores, sit in a hotel lobby, walk along Fifth Avenue, coffee at Bickford's, sit in a hotel lobby, walk along Broadway, and then the weary trek home to inform her mother that the search for work was no joke.

She could have secured many jobs. There was that typing job in a real estate office, a packer at Saks, a file clerk with a mail order house, but she scorned all jobs, all jobs.

The stress of working in the city meant the harsh sentence of being committed to a penitentiary under a warden named mother, a penitentiary with its daily pressure of a mother flapping wings over her reflections, laboring to zipper her behavior, straining to puff out her physical relish for joy. *Mother, may I go out prancing? No, my darling daughter! Mother, may I stay home moping? Yes, oh, yes, my darling daughter!*

She had tried to fight this deathless execution of her mother's plan through the suffocating years of her slow childhood, her brief classroom of adolescence, her hard and compact maturity, and now, at long last, the birth of protest and slick mutiny, amen, and now the plan was minus its surge and decaying at its base, amen. *Am I blue, am I blue, ain't these tears in my eyes telling you?*

The rapture of going to Washington was like a lit candle warming her bones, and not being called at once made her hiss their way of doing things. *Hell hath no fury like a citizen scorned.* But she lived under the gay halo of knowing that the telegram would soon arrive in a tan envelope, and it was like guzzling a dizzy beverage and dancing over tall glasses of scotch and soda.

She strolled into a department store, fingered their fabulous articles, asked the salesgirls for merchandise she knew they didn't have, rode up and down the elevators and up and down the escalators and out of the store and into the hotel across the street.

An enjoyment cloaked her when the bellhops stared at her, and the men in the chairs forsook the editorial page to ogle her knees. She sat in a soft chair and lit a cigaret. *Where do they go, these smokerings I blow?*

A man approached her and asked if Lucy Edison was her name.

She said: Oh, no! I'm Madame Z, the last word.

The man faked a laugh and asked if she'd have coffee with him in the tea room. The aroma of coffee smelled rich and lazy, and they entered the tea room for coffee.

She said: Lucy Edison. Tell me all about Lucy Edison.

The man said: Oh, she's a girl I knew who used to wear blue flowers in her hair.

She said: Go on, I'll bet she was your third wife, the one you murdered in the bathtub.

The man said: Oh, she's really unimportant, very dull and routine. Tell me about yourself. Don't leave out one detail.

She said: No, you tell me, was this Edison girl the light of your life?

The man said: Edison, the light of my life. Good gag. Heh, heh, heh.

They ambled into the arena of cliches about the weather, the price of eggs and if the production of babies during wartime was the right thing to do, and the man asked if she'd at all mind if they went to his room where he'd appreciate her opinion of his engineering blueprints, and the conversation committed suicide on that note.

She said: Blueprints thrill me, but I am sorry. You see, I am to meet Mother and Dad. We're to go furniture shopping. Dad bought a home on Long Island, you know.

A twitch moved the man's mouth out of shape, and he said: well, you can't shoot me at dawn for trying.

She said: How would the night do?

The man paid the check and they left the tea room, he to his newspaper, she to the revolving door where the doorman asked if she'd like a cab.

She said: My good man, don't be ridic! This is God's day for walking.

The doorman tipped his cap and said: yes, Ma'm.

Mabel headed toward Fifth Avenue and the shops, routine number three.

Two men passed and one of them smiled at her and she matched his smile. The man quit his friend to join her.

He said: My name's Chasman. And yours?

She said: How do you do, Mr. Chasman. My name's Lucy Edison.

He said: How do you do, Miss Edison. And where is Miss Edison going this very fine morning?

She said: Mrs. Edison is going to meet her husband this very fine morning in exactly ten minutes. Would Mr. Chasman like to come along to meet Mr. Edison? He's such a fine fellow, my husband.

He said: No, thank you, Mrs. Edison, Mr. Chasman is in no physical condition to meet husbands this very fine morning. Especially in ten minutes.

She said: Oh, what a shame. Why, you'd love Mr. Edison. He's a wrestler, so big and strong.

Mr. Chasman quickly paid his loving respect to her husband, the wrestler, and walked to his friend, who was pacing before a delicatessen. Mabel reached Fifth Avenue alone. *Oh, heaven help the working girl on a morning like this.*

She scanned the shop windows for the things she would love to buy, passed the Public Library and someone whistled to her from a parked bus. She turned to see a grinning sailor with missing teeth. *Join the Navy and see your dentist.*

A mink-coated girl walked by her, scraped a ream of phlegm from her throat, unloaded it on the sidewalk and turned down the block.

That's an aristocrat for you, all right. Isn't the gutter good enough for her?

An inertia swallowed her, and she wondered: where to now? She rummaged her brain for new hotels to flop in. She remembered that silky band over the radio coming from the Hotel St. Moritz. The Hotel St. Moritz. Delicious name. Swank taste. Never been there before. What sort of lobby have they? Soft lights? Soft chairs? And what sort of newspapers do the men read, and what color uniform do the bellhops wear, and how is their eyesight this morning? And would the silky band be playing this morning? *Dancing in the dark, with someone's true-love I'm dancing in the dark.* Well, she'd take a crack at it. Yes, she'd take a crack at it, all right. Taking cracks at any old thing was her meat.

A wind inflated the avenue and she strode off to her destination unknown with her mind strumming over the opulent rhapsody of ditching New York for Washington, her pie in the sky, her place in the sun, her own place, her own place to come and go, her own and only her own, her own lock, stock and bed, her triumph to bottle, but, as yet, a sloppy victory.

A stucco of agony clothed her mind when she thought of having to go home to see her mother at home, a frail compound of maudlin substance. Her mother, the holy Mother Superior, commissioned by God to enroll her as a nun in the Convent of the Lower Depths.

Swing low, sweet BMT, coming for to carry me home.

Someone shut the warm faucet in her body, and she quaked in the wind.

A man on a motorcycle tooted his horn, and she heard a boy call his father a jerk.

CHAPTER 4

THE USHER spotted their struggle to crash the movies and they sprinted down the street and into a 5-and-10 where Joe robbed a tube of toothpaste and Jelly robbed a woman's bandanna. *They float through the street with the greatest of ease, the daring young men.*

They were wearing baseball caps and Joe had a baseball glove on his left hand, and as they rambled along he punched his right fist into the pocket of the glove.

Joe said: Hey, Jelly, got any goddamn money?

Jelly said: Twelve cents.

Joe said: Call that money?

Jelly said: How much you got?

Joe said: Goddamn nothing, that's what I got.

Jelly said: Wotta we gonna do, Joe?

Joe said: Wanna try the movies again?

Jelly said: But the usher's wise.

Joe said: Oh, ain't he one dirty punk!

Jelly said: Wanna look up Piano Leg Mary?

Joe said: Oh, that goddamn dumb broad!

Jelly said: So wottayawanna do, Joe?

Joe said: Wish we had pockets fulla dough.

Jelly said: Supposing we had, Joe?

Joe said: We'd go to the poolroom and shoot a game.

Jelly said: Jesus, Joe, you know Mister B says we're too young. How many times must he tell us? Jesus, I don't wanna hear over and over that I'm a punk kid, too young to shoot pool. I got feelings, Joe.

Joe said: And I ain't got feelings, I suppose? How do you think I feel? Well, I'm gonna tell you how I feel. I feel like two cents, that's how I feel!

Jelly said: So wottayawanna go to Mister B for?

Joe said: Maybe he'll say okay this time. Can't tell about human nature, Jelly.

Jelly said: Aw, Joe!

Joe said: Don't Joe me! You wanna come? Yes or no?

Jelly said: So wottaya blowing your top for? You know I'll go, Joe.

Joe said: See this lady coming our way? Gimme the bandanna you swiped.

Jelly said: But I robbed it for my mother.

Joe said: Look, Jelly, sons don't rob things for their mothers! So gimme the bandanna and I'll put in my toothpaste and I'll ask the goddamn sucker if she wannsa buy it. Here she comes. Now, don't talk. Keep your yap shut.

A woman strolled by clutching a magazine and a cat, and Joe stepped up to her, his face and eyes a study in gloom.

Dearly beloved lady, how clearly I see, somewhere in heaven you were fashioned for me.

He said: Gee, lady, can I please touch your beautiful cat?

She said: Why, of course.

He said: We hadda cat like that once. It was like our own flesh and blood. But Mom hadda send it away 'cause we had no money to buy milk and liver for it. Ain't that a pity, lady?

She said: Ah, poor tiny boy.

He said: And now every time I see a cat I wanna pet it and think it's our own little Tootsy. But I think your cat's prettier than Tootsy, even though Tootsy won prizes.

She said: Why, thank you so awfully.

He said: Mom's all broken up about sending Tootsy away, and don't think she'd do it if she had money. And, gee, Mom's always crying about Tootsy. Sometimes I cry, too.

She said: Ah, how ghastly.

Joe said: Why Mom's so poor she even gave me her own dead mother's beautiful bandanna and our only tube of toothpaste to see if me and my deaf and dumb brother over there can sell it. I asked lottsa people, but I guess lottsa people don't care if other people are flat on their backs. I guess that's life, huh, lady?

She said: Well, don't you dare think all people are like that. I'll buy your bandanna and toothpaste.

He said: Oh, lady, you're a kind lady.

She said: How much do you want for the bandanna?

He said: Well, Mom says it's been inna family for eighty years and it comes from Alaska, and Mom even went and washed it and pressed it so it should look beautiful. And you know what else? I think it's just the right color for you.

She said: Will fifty cents do?

He said: Can you make it seventy-five cents, please?

She said: Why, of course I can. Here, you hold Tangerine while I get you the money.

Roses are red, violets are blue, people are chumps, you, too.

She poked into her bag and extracted the sum and gave it to Joe.

She said: Mind you, I'll just take the bandanna, but you keep the toothpaste for you and your brother to brush your teeth every day and every night. Promise you will?

He said: I swear to God, lady. Every day and every night.

She said: Well, goodbye, young man, and I hope your mother gets her Tootsy back.

He said: Gee, it's sure nice for you to say that. Well, goodbye. Goodbye, Tangerine. Goodbye.

The woman strolled away with the slushy smile of a philanthropic saint, and Joe said to Jelly that the goddamn cat smelled like holy hell and sprinkled over his hands, and that if it was up to him he'd strangle every goddamn one of them, every goddamn one of them. Including that stinking Tangerine.

Jelly said: Joe, you're hot. I gotta hand it to you.

Joe said: I'll tell you the truth, Jelly. Women are so goddamn dumb.

Jelly said: So do we go half onna sale, Joe?

Joe said: What? You rob it for nothing and I sell what you robbed for nothing for seventy-five cents and you want half! That's how much you're wise on business deals! Here's fifteen cents!

Jelly said: Aw, cut it out, Joe Did I open my yap when you said I was deaf and dumb?

Joe said: Take the goddamn fifteen cents or you get goddamn nothing!

Jelly said: I'll take the fifteen cents.

Joe gave him a slice of the loot, and they headed across the avenue to the poolroom, Joe punching his fist into his glove and Jelly muttering something about it being a lowdown, dirty shame, him being the victim of one helleva dirty deal.

BEETHOVEN'S POOL PARLOR

CLUB FOR GENTLEMEN

POOL: 40C PER HOUR

CHICAGO: 10C PER GAME

MAKE THIS YOUR HOME

They skipped down the stairs and the poolroom slapped their eyes with its garish shine of green cloth and ivory balls, and they squirted gluey awe at the posters advertising dances, prizefights, cigarets, and they seemed to collectively swoon before the spicy nudes gracing the beer and whiskey ads. Two men were shooting pool in the back of the room, and Beethoven, Mister B, was sandpapering poolstick tips.

Joe said: Hello, Mister B. How are you feeling?

Mister B said: You down here again?

Joe said: How's Mrs. B?

Mister B said: How many times must I tell you you're too young and you can't shoot pool in my place?

Joe said: Aw, Mister B, me and Jelly just came down to pay you a visit and maybe drink a soda.

Mister B said: How come you come down here for a soda whenna streets are fulla soda joints?

Joe said: How do I know why? Am I a philosopher?

The intermission was over and Mister B resumed his work, and Joe nudged Jelly to vamoose, get lost. Jelly edged toward the men at the pooltable, and Joe eased up to Mister B.

Joe said: Guess you gotta know science to fix poolsticks, huh,

Mister B?

Mister B said: Outside it's cold. Baseball's a summer game. How come you're wearing a cap and a glove when it's cold outside?

Joe said: Is there a law against playing baseball inna wind, Mister B?

Mister B said: Baseball's a game I can do without.

Joe said: Baseball's America's great sport.

Mister B said: I like fishing. Fishing's my sport.

Joe said: You just try counting alla fans going to baseball games, Mister B.

Mister B said: I was a wonderful fisherman.

Joe said: Babe Ruth was a man of the people.

Mister B said: People usta say: Mister B, get smart. Get outa the poolroom and get rich fishing.

Joe said: Excuse me, Mister B, but if you hate baseball you hate Babe Ruth.

Mister B said: Off the coast of Maine I caught fish as big as men.

Joe said: Well, all I gotta say it's un-American to hate Babe Ruth.

Mister B said: In Cuba I always wanted to fish.

Joe said: Onna level, Mister B, wottaya got against Babe Ruth?

Mister B said: In Cuba the fishes are giants.

Joe said: Did Babe Ruth do you any harm?

Mister B said: I love to fish, but, oh, my God, I hate to eat fish.

Joe said: I'm surprised at your attitude, Mister B.

Mister B said: People should eat what they catch.

Joe said: I just can't get over your attitude, that's all.

Mister B said: It's the smell of fish I can't stand.

Joe said: If I didn't like you so much I'd tell you to get outa town.

Mister B said: When fish is cooked my stomach turns.

Joe said: Seeing it's you, I'll straighten you out on baseball.

Mister B said: To my brother I'd give the fish I caught.

Joe said: After all, Mister B, you're a personal pal of mine.

Mister B said: Sometimes I'd throw the fish back into the sea.

Joe said: I liked you the minute I saw you.

Mister B said: It kills me to say it, but I don't fish anymore.

Joe said: I was telling my friends just the other day what a real nice man you are.

Mister B said: Not being able to fish anymore tears my heart out.

Joe said: It's this way, Mister B. Babe Ruth made seventy-five thousand a year.

Mister B said: I can cry when I see men go off to fish.

Joe said: They don't pay the President more than that.

Mister B said: It cost money to fish.

Joe said: I leave it to you, a fair man, is that salary tin?

Mister B said: My boy, inna world we live in you gotta pay for what you love to do.

Joe said: Maybe, Mister B, after the war things'll change.

Mister B said: Makes no difference. Paying for what you love to do is an important part of the law.

Joe said: Laws, laws! From me to you, my friend, there's too many goddamn laws!

Mister B said: Congress oughta pass a law saying people don't hafta pay for what they love to do.

Joe spit into the pocket of his glove and rammed his fist into the spit, and said: Ain't it funny how we think the same about those goddamn laws?

Mister B said: Why did you just spit in your glove? Are you crazy?

Joe said: Spit makes the leather soft, Mister B.

Mister B said: That idea's one crazy idea, all right.

Joe said: About those laws, Mister B.

Mister B said: Spitting breeds germs. I can't stand germs.

Joe said: Hey, Mister B, so wottsa little germ?

Mister B said: Sit down! You're rocking the boat!

Joe said: To get back to those laws, Mister B.

Mister B said: And wottahell about those laws?

Joe said: Well, we've been talking like old friends about these laws and I see it bothers you like it bothers me, and it's a good thing for friends to get things off their chest. Now, pal, you take that law hanging next to the lady with nothing on, and it says guys under sixteen can't shoot pool here, and I guess that's one law you and me can't goddamn stand, huh, pal?

Mister B said: Goddamn you! Wanna get me arrested! Wanna take away my bread and butter? Wanna see me inna street begging?

Joe said: Take it easy, pal. Have a heart. But didn't you say to hell with those goddamn laws?

Mister B said: Well, wottahellaya waiting for? Beat it!

Joe said: Wanna tube of toothpaste, Mister B?

Mister B said: Get outa here and get your friend outa here and stay outa here!

Joe said: Okay, Mister B, if that's the way you treat customers me and my friend'll take our business elsewhere.

Mister B said: Go home and grow up!

Joe said: Hey, Jelly! Come on! Mister B ain't interested in our cash. Mister B ain't even interested in my toothpaste. You can't tell, Mister B, maybe Mrs. B might like the brand.

Mister B said: Gettahelloutahere!

It's a pity old age is wasted on the old.

Joe and Jelly plodded up the stairs, and Joe cursed his father for not marrying his mother sooner, and he swore at Mother Nature for taking her goddamn time about releasing his license to grow up more quickly. Jelly underlined Joe's communique to all existing parties.

I regret that I have but one life to give to my poolroom.

Jelly said: Hey, Joe, wottayawanna do?

Joe said: I'll tell you what I'd like to goddamn do!

Jelly said: What, Joe?

Joe said: Strap that goddamn sonuva Mister B to a tree, rip alla laws right in that puss of his and stuff cooked fish down his mouth all day long! And I'll tell you something else. Listen, Jelly. What I'm gonna tell you is the truth. It's guys like Mister B that starts alla wars!

Jelly said: There's Piano Leg Mary.

Joe said: Hey, Piano Leg!

A squat, dumpy girl in gym bloomers ran up to them.

She said: Want me, Joe?

Joe said: Piano Leg, if you don't do me a favor I'm sunk.

She said: But, Joe, ain't I always doing you favors?

Joe said: See this toothpaste? Well, I went and bought it at the five and dime and I brought it home and, oh, hell, Mom gave me one goddamn bawling out for buying the wrong brand, and I know the five and dime ain't got the brand Mom wants, and, well, Piano Leg, you know good and well how I hate like hell to ask for my goddamn money back, and seeing you're one of my real close friends, I wonder if you'd prove it by getting my money back just so I don't hafta catch hell from Mom.

She said: Joe, of course I'll do it! How would it look if I didn't do my buddy from away back such a little favor? Gimme the toothpaste. Be right back.

Mary, Mary, quite contrary, how does your piano leg grow?

They watched Mary speed down the street, her gym bloomers swinging in the wind, and Joe said to Jelly: Jelly, there's two things I hate this goddamn minute—Mister B for throwing up my goddamn age in my face and those goddamn piano legs running down the street!

Youth in the raw is seldom mild.

Joe said: After you finish picking your nose how about chipping in for cigarets and smoking them onna roof?

CHAPTER 5

IT WAS the morning after the night Chesty had told him that he was slated for the Army in three or four months, the morning after a long, jangling night of psychotic chaos, and the old man went off to work, the pulp of his insides bobbing and weaving like a fighter gone berserk. The old man wore his medals, a fluttering ribbon of purple heartaches.

This is the way it should be, they say. They say every boy is needed. Well, sure they're needed and, damnit, they're going and they're coming and they're fighting and they're winning and, Jesus, they're dying. So okay. So okay I'm a dirty slacker because I'm bawling about my son going away. I'm a no good heel because I know the world's in one helluva state and I know there's gotta be young guys to murder the bastards who're murdering the young guys and their ideas on how the world should be run. And get a good look at me sounding off against Chesty leaving and maybe never coming back, and maybe being buried in some strange place where men and women with funny names live and work. But I say it's this way and you'll say, but it's that way, but I say it's this way on account of me being a goner without my son to look at and hope for. I'm part of this big world and Chesty's a big part of me, and I need him, and I know bigger things than me need him, and that's what makes the whole frigging thing stink on packed ice because I'm so damn wet and wrong. And I know goddamn well if I met a guy right this minute who'd come up to me and sound off with the bellyache that I'm going through, why, I'd haul off and kick his guts in, and then I'd tell this guy wottahell does he think this war is, a goddamn waltz? And then I'd see if he had anymore guts left to kick in. Tell me I oughta look at it that way and I'd tell you you're right, you're right, and here's my hand on it. But go ahead and swing me to a tree and I'll still bawl I'm dead without Chesty, and with Chesty I can walk straight. And soon he'll be going away and I know the Army'll be proud of him and I'll be proud of him. But if you say, Mister, you look like you're dying, I'll say, Mac, you ain't kidding. Oh, ain't it a helluva miserable hell to know you're wrong and they're right, and to know with all you got in you that you'll just hafta get usta the idea of walking around dead?

He reached the factory, his mind soaked in a muddy pit. He entered the freight elevator and Phil, the operator, said something to him and the men in the bulky loft said something to him, and Rority at the next bench was crying, but the old man tramped through the numb and automatic project of a man who knew his job and wasn't detoured by neighboring grief, a simple John Doe sliding up and down the emotional thermometer of organic scenes dramatized in his own private wasteland, a classified robot at work.

Some of the men, like Busa, Kamrowski and Russell, extended platters of advice to Rority, who was struggling to button up a sack of tears.

Busa said: Why don't you go home, Rority?

Russell said: Sure, take the day off. Go to a movie and sit inna dark.

Kamrowski said: That's what I do when things go wrong.

Russell said: Nothing like a dark movie when things go wrong.

Kamrowski said: You gotta hand it to the movies, all right.

Busa said: It's tough, Rority. If there's anything I can do, Rority.

Russell said: Want me to tella foreman you wanna go home?

Kamrowski said: Foreman's a good egg. He'll okay it. Rority broke through his burden and shook his small head.

Busa said: Sure, maybe work'll make you forget a little. Lemme know if you need a hand.

Kamrowski said: He oughta go to a movie.

Russell said: That's what I always do.

The three returned to their machines. Rority hid his eyes behind his shirtsleeve.

Busa said: Look at that Anderson. Ain't he a cool punk. Here Rority loses a son inna South Pacific and sits right by him crying like a kid and Anderson works with a diaper pin on his lips. Oh, Christ!

Kamrowski said: But you gotta hand it to those cool guys, born without hearts. They say to hell with you and hurray for me, and sometimes I'd give my right arm to be a member of that tribe.

Busa said: You can have it! Gimme the guys who can laugh and cry and that's the human race I'm a part of! To hell with the cold, brave men!

Russell said: There's all kinds of people. But if we don't start working we'll get canned. And then what?

Trouble's just a bubble and the clouds will soon roll by. . . .

The broken jargon of the machines, and its rattling vibration in concert with the battering hammers and the buzz of the saws, trapped every board of the silent floor, and the metallic weapons for American defense and offense ran the mechanized gamut from the crude to the refined. Three Army officers were talking to a man in a blue serge suit, and the men at the benches tuned their eyes and hands to the whirring chant of humming screws and bolts. A fat girl came into the shop calling for a Major Telson: wanted on the phone.

Spasms of moody nuances stamped its print into Rority, and he tried very hard not to think of his one child, his son, his son at home, his son at war, his son dead in an unpronounceable part of the globe. He tried to barricade his memory behind the necessity of things to do, and he tried to dismiss the growth of his son and how he proudly measured every inch of his growth. And there was that summer day his son brought home a pretty girl and laughed and asked his father and mother to meet the girl he was going to marry, and they all laughed and ate apples and laughed some more, and his son kissed the girl and the girl drooped her eyes and they laughed again, and the girl lifted her eyes and joined them.

Rority's hope of a barricade became dented and shot full of holes, and he wondered if his son's girl would be capable of laughter anymore, and he laid his head down on his and bench and wept, and his hand fell under his machine and a blade sliced away two of his fingers, and the men coiled a rope of pity around him, and the Army majors and the man in the blue serge suit carried him away, and the fat girl called for an ambulance, and the men went back to their benches.

Busa said: Oh, Jesus Christ!

Russell said: Dammit, couldn't he've gone home? Did he hafta stay here?

Kamrowski said: A movie would've been the best thing.

Busa said: Oh, that rotten Hitler and the rotten men who made him! Goddamn their rotten souls! Do you hear? Goddamn their rotten souls!

The foreman said: Okay, men, if you wanna get rid of Hitler you'll hafta run the machines. Let's get to work.

No time for tragedy.

The men at the benches once again conducted the symphony of the machines, and the momentary pause was purged, and the old man's machine broke down. The foreman came over to analyze the trouble, and the old man hoped he'd hurry, since a stoppage at work meant the wiring of his thoughts to Chesty, and there was Chesty standing before him as big as life, and he walked to the window and saw the taut canyons of Manhattan stabbing their fingers into the white pillows of the sky, and he turned to the foreman and cursed him for taking so long, and cursed the machine for the few minutes of liberty to think of things he had no heart for.

Hurry, for God's sake, hurry, will you? Do you think it's easy standing here and thinking of a piece of you leaving you?

The foreman said: Okay, Anderson

The old man went back to his bench, his discharge from the chambers of his inner strife. He started his machine and the roar blasted apart his mental wanderings, and the morning turned to noon, and the factory windows felt the blare of a strong sun, and its gold paint polished the oily walls, and the lunch-hour whistle blew, and the machines lost their clatter, and the human voice replaced the voice of the machine.

Kamrowski said: Where are you eating, Anderson?

The old man said: At Bill's Place.

Kamrowski said: Want company?

The old man said: Sounds good.

They stepped into the elevator.

Kamrowski said: Tough on Rority, huh?

The old man said: Rority? George Rority?

Kamrowski said: Who the hellaya think I mean?

The elevator stopped at the street level.

The old man said: Why, what happened to George?

Kamrowski said: Look, Anderson, is it okay with you if I don't eat with you? We'll make it some other day, okay? Someday when I feel icy and cold. Know what I mean? So long, Anderson! Nice knowing you!

The old man watched Kamrowski rush along the curb.

Oh, hell, haven't I got enough troubles of my own without that big lemon starting one more batch? And what about Rority? What's happened to him that sets Kamrowski on fire? Well, I'm gonna see Rority when I get back. You're damn right I will.

He hoped Bill's Place had pot roast on its blue-plate special, and he wondered if Rority would be eating at Bill's.

Am I my brother's keeper?

CHAPTER 6

THE SUNDAY afternoon was bleak and the concrete sky allowed the sun to peep upon the earth through a narrow slit, and groups of men were laced together by waxed conversation. A beggar trudged in and out of the entrances and exits moving his heavy lips. A weary boy fidgeted between two loud women in seedy coats. Three soldiers were watching a girl take a shine. A chubby pigeon strutted around the rim of a water fountain that wasn't running, and a lame man spit at a tree.

The meek shall inherit the park.

The old man and Joe, and Skinny and Chesty lumbered along the cement path, and Chesty saw a girl and an old lady walking by. He looked at the girl and the girl looked at the old face of the lady, swashed in white powder over tired lines, and the girl strode on and the old lady hobbled on, and Chesty felt sorry for the girl's pimply face.

The old man said: How about sitting down?

Skinny and Chesty sat opposite the old man and Joe, and Skinny wished he had a football to kick along the naked spaces between the crooked trees. Joe's tongue counted three holes in his teeth.

Chesty said: I don't see Petey Malenko anymore.

Skinny said: Petey's father gotta job in Detroit. Petey went along.

Chesty said: Do you miss him?

Yes, he missed Petey Malenko, his great and wonderful friend with the funny crosseyes. He left for Detroit six months ago, and he had been missing him for six months, twenty-four weeks, and he had been walking and walking in this park by the river for six months, twenty-four weeks, his young body swollen with the vital curiosity if he'd ever find another Petey Malenko, and if Petey Malenko missed him as much he missed Petey Malenko.

He said: I miss Petey, and I wonder if he'll ever come back.

Chesty said: Maybe he will. Maybe he'll come back next spring.

But next spring was next year, and the days are blue and the nights are black, and he was troubled over how he was going to live until the next year without a friend, and he wondered if he would die before the next year without a friend. *Application for a friend.*

He said: Petey was my buddy, my only buddy.

Chesty said: Guess it's tough without a buddy.

Skinny dug his hands into his pockets and was able to feel his flesh through the holes in his pockets. He hunched his shoulders when the midday air developed a new crispness, and a poster on a billboard caught his eye. *Uncle Sam Needs You.* He liked the old man in the tall high hat and the long white beard. He hoped he'd look like that someday. He wondered who the old man was pointing at.

Chesty said: Look at Joe, the people's friend. He'll never grow lonely.

Skinny said: Everybody knows Joe. Wherever you go they say: where's Joe, what's he doing, when's he coming around? Joe, Joe, Joe. Wherever you go it's Joe.

Chesty said: What do you do when school ends?

Skinny said: Oh, I walk around, go home, do my homework, walk around, go home to eat, and I walk around some more.

Chesty said: By yourself?

Skinny said: I just told you Petey was my only buddy.

A sigh sneaked through Skinny's nose and mouth, and Chesty peered at his brother and tried to study him as he always tried to study him, as he always longed to arrange his symptoms in neat cubicles and x-ray each one of them, but the stubborn backwash of his own tight plight stymied, and he gave up the study as he always gave up the study. He lit a cigaret, and Skinny wondered how he'd feel with a cigaret stuck out of his lips.

I can't give you anything but love, Skinny. *That's the only thing I've plenty of,* Skinny.

Joe was entertaining a ticking spleen, and he knew that if the old man didn't stop gaping across at Chesty he'd explode and stain the park with bloody body fragments. In the last few days he felt he was being trapped in a net of farewells and tears. His mother sobbed all through the night over the telegram Mabel received from Washington, and he tossed in his bed and heard Mabel sing gay songs in the bathroom. And now it was the old man and Chesty, the same words, the same music.

Oh, Pop, be yourself. The Army's got ten million guys and Chesty makes it an odd ten million and one. And wottahellaya see in that goddamn wise guy? Oh, maybe you think I'm just a snotty kid, born last Thursday, but I'm a helluva lot older than you think. I gotta pretty good idea why you've been looking at that guy for years like he was Miss America. If he was a guy looking for action, if he had one goddamn chip on his shoulder, why, I'd say, okay, Pop, that's your boy and forget me. But he's a tired mouse and it eats me up to see my favorite old man betting onna wrong horse. And I wanna say something else: it ain't easy to feel like a goddamn orphan whenever he's around. And I wanna say that I ain't got an icebox for a heart, you know. You've been dishing it out, Pop, and I've been taking it, but goddamn, Pop, take it easy!

The old man said: Look at him, Joe. Look at those legs, those shoulders, those big hands. Look, Joe, look at the guts in his face.

Joe said: This is where I came in.

And now I lay me down to growl, and pray the Lord my soul to howl.

An irritation blistered Chesty and he wanted to crawl out of the old man's smacking stare examining him and his possibilities for use and wear, and he felt like some cheap trinket ready to be snatched from a bargain counter. He tried to recollect the birth of the stock appraisal that grew with the days of his life. There were many looming episodes, too many for him to certify its unimmaculate conception. He thought of the secret peepshow maintained by his patron, the old man, and how he often watered his flame to appease the old man's lust to feast upon his body. He thought of the night the old man spoke of his life and its tawdry glory and its decorative layers of aches. He was told of the leading role he was to perform in the wholesale carnival, created the day he was extracted from the womb. And then came the lean days, the days of smothering his face in his hands and trying not to cry out of a weak mouth, the days he spoke so tenderly to the old man, the days he railed against the old man's demand to display his growth. And then came the fat day he had discovered the strange colony that read books.

Chesty-in-Wonderland.

It was snowing and a storm mangled the streets, and he retreated into a library on a corner and saw a book written by a Sherwood Anderson. He liked the rosy glow of reading something by a man with his name. The stories he read concerned the life and death of sensitive people in a small town. And from this initiation came his romance with the written word and the deluge of other writers and their works and worth, and from their fluid ideas he unwrapped a home-made microscope with which to scan the old man. At first he groped, but then he was able to touch and understand the old man's concept of life and how it should be run according to schedule, and he knew that he was not the chosen one to handle the alien reins, and that there was a fuming discord in their duet, the old man was singing hallelujah while he was droning a dirge.

He looked at the old man and met his wink and smile.

Do you take this father to be your lawful wedded wife? I don't!

Joe gazed at the sky and around the park and saw the lanky apartment houses, snobbish and severe in their tailored trousseau of chic towers, and Skinny followed Joe's gaze and felt stunted and afraid before the architectural dinosaurs. Joe turned to Skinny and resented his scanty diagram of bones and flesh.

He said: Hey, Pop, how the goddamn did Skinny creep into our family?

The old man said: Well, isn't that one helluva thing to say about your kid brother!

He said: Behave, Pop! All I wanna know is who invited him?

The old man said: The same people who invited you!

He said: Okay, Pop, I get the idea. This is a free country and the good comes with the bad.

The old man said: I like you, Joe. I like Skinny, too. I like all my kids. But don't you holler at me about who should be here and who shouldn't!

He said: Hey, take it easy, will you, Pop?

The old man said: It's tough enough losing Chesty and Mom losing Mabel without you laying it on!

He said: Onna level, Pop, wottaya want from Chesty?

The old man said: I'll send you a letter!

He said: I'm no dumb slob, you know. I got ideas what you want from Chesty!

The old man said: So you're a big boy now! You know what's playing!

He said: I can take your gaff, Pop. I'm hard alla way through. But lemme say this: supposing you don't get what you want from Chesty? Then what?

The old man said: Oh, Joe, you're my kid. I don't wanna fight with my kid. But you're throwing the bull right in your old man's face. So don't gimme that junk. Chesty's me and blood's blood. Chesty'll get around to what I want, wait and see. Hell, just look at him and you're seeing me. Joe, I'm a great believer in this blood business.

Chesty said: Does the teacher ever read poetry to you kids?

Skinny said: If a man by the name of Henry Wadsworth Long-fellow writes that stuff then she reads it on Friday only.

Chesty said: What do you think of it.

Skinny said: I don't understand it.

Chesty said: I write poetry. I should say, I wrote a poem.
Skinny said: Yeah, Chesty?
Chesty said: Want to hear it?
Skinny said: Think I'll understand it?
Chesty fished a white paper from his coat and said: maybe you
will.

I PLEDGE ALLEGIANCE TO THE PALE GIRLS
    a yellow horn
       ripped
          the smoky moon
    and
       the page girls
         studied
           the pale girls.

    dark hands at 3 A.M.
       caressed
         white keys,
    a guitar
       plucked
         a wall.

    a door opened . . .
       and
         the yellow horn
           stood to greet
              the open door—

    two girls in red
       entered
         and
           flitted

                                their
                                    perfumed
                                        bodies
                        and
                            studied
                                the pale girls
                                    who
                                        studied
                                            the pale girls,
                            and
                                the yellow horn
                                    sat
                                        and
                                            sobbed.

the bartender called it the blues.

Skinny said: The pale girls . . .
Chesty said: What?
Skinny said: Nothing, Chesty, nothing.
Chesty said: Like it?
Skinny said: It ain't like Henry Wadsworth Longfellow.

Joe said: You could put in your right eye what I know about blood, Pop, but if it's okay with you it's Jake with me.

The old man said: A man once said blood's thicker than water. I take my hat off to that man.

Joe said: But maybe if that man gotta load of Skinny he'd throw his hands in the air and say he gives up.

The old man said: You sounding off again, Joe?

Joe said: Hey, Pop, what did I say?

The old man said: Oh, Joe, do me a favor and close that trap of yours!

Joe said: All I goddamn said was something about Skinny and you tear my head off.

The old man said: Shut up, Joe! You hear?

Joe said: I hear.

Skinny said: You know something, Chesty? Joe never speaks to me.

Chesty said: How come?

Skinny said: I dunno. Honest I don't. I think Joe hates me.

He wanted to say that Joe never spoke to him, that if Joe wanted to say anything, why, he'd yell at him, always yelling. He wanted to say that he yelled back, but his yelling went on inside of him, always going on inside of him. He wanted to say that once he was alone, and he saw Joe and his friends, and he was so glad to see Joe, and he went up to him and said: hello, Joe. But Joe walked away without saying anything, and one of his friends said: hey, Joe, that was your brother! And Joe hit his friend in the teeth and went on walking, and that he felt sick in the street. He wanted to say these things to Chesty. He felt Chesty would understand, but he didn't say anything, and he yelled at himself inside of him for not opening his mouth to let the yelling flow out.

A dog sniffed at Chesty's leg.

I can tell you lottsa things, Chesty, things you don't know about 'cause you're never around to know. One thing I'll tell you is that Joe's always saying dirty things about me in front of me, and it's all about the way I look. But I'll tell you this, Chesty. Someday I ain't gonna let Joe say these things. I'm gonna make him stop once and for all. See if I don't. Maybe I don't know when that day's gonna come, but it's gonna come. Joe's not gonna yell at me anymore after that day. And when I see him inna street he'll say hello and he ain't gonna bust his friend inna teeth just because he was reminded I was his brother. Maybe me and Joe'll be friends when that day comes. Real good friends.

Chesty said: Well, some sweet day Joe will understand a lot more than he does now. Maybe that day's worth waiting for. In a way I'm waiting for that kind of sweet day myself. Tell you what: we'll call that the Emancipation Proclamation. How's that?

The Emancipation Proclamation.

The meaning of the phrase held no clarity for Skinny, but the sound and clear ring of it agitated him and braced him with an anxiety that made him tremble a little and giggle a little. A man walked by puffing on a pipe, and Skinny wondered how he'd feel with a pipe stuck out of his lips.

A crew of birds chattered and poured life into a limp tree, and the sky sealed its slit and jailed the sun, and the old man thought it illegal for the sun not to shine on Sunday. The low moan of a wind yawned across the park, and Joe said his belly was talking.

The old man called out to Chesty: Think we'd better go. Chances are that dinner's onna table.

Three children ran and leaped in the grass with their mother's plea to please be careful lashed to their pink ears, and the male wing of the Anderson tribe picked up their bodies to go home for dinner.

The old man strolled between Chesty and Joe, and Skinny moved before them, his feet devoted to walk the straight-lined vein in the cement.

Onward Christian soldiers, marching off to eat.

CHAPTER 7

THE BULB in Mabel's head glowed brightly and Mrs. Anderson was mashing potatoes. They were preparing the traditional Sunday dinner. Mabel whistled while she peeled onions.

Mrs. Anderson said: Oh, God, Mabel, must you whistle?

Mabel said: And what's the matter with you?

Mrs. Anderson said: Well, I think, dear, this no time to whistle.

Mabel said: Forgive me, mother, for being happy!

Mrs. Anderson said: Oh, dear Mabel, when I went shopping yesterday I saw that awful blonde woman walking her pooch, and you know where she gets the money to buy her clothes and pay her rent. And I thought of you and I thanked dear God I took care of you the way I did. And now you're going away. Oh, Mabel, who will take care of you in Washington, and why do you whistle?

Mabel said: I wonder what will happen to that blonde and her pooch when her lovers run out of gravy?

Mrs. Anderson said: Mabel, mother is talking. Who will take care of you in Washington?

Mabel said: Oh, I'm so positive that God will!

Mrs. Anderson said: Mabel, Mabel, must you go away?

Yes, Mabel must go away. If Mabel doesn't go away Mabel shall crack her lungs with terrible screams. And would dear Mother want to see dear Mabel suffering from cracked lungs?

Mabel said: I just haven't the guts to go into what you've been wringing dry since that telegram came. I'm going to rest my bones until the storm blows over.

Mrs. Anderson watched Mabel open the bedroom door, and the slam of the door shook the floor under her. She tried to bind her energies to the mold of food before her, but an intimate pain flung its sting in and around her chest, and a weakness licked into her, and she sat by the window, and her long fingers drummed a slow beat against the window pane while she took her thoughts for a walk through familiar corridors. She remembered her first introduction to her daughter.

The nurse said: Here's your baby, Mrs. Anderson.

And she looked at her baby, a few pounds of scrubbed flesh with no hair and creased eyes. The nurse left the room and she was alone and felt the blunt terror she had stored-up for this first meeting melt and drift away.

Your name is Mabel. I'm your mother and you're my daughter, and your father will soon be here to meet you. Your second name is Anderson. This is a hospital in East St. Louis.

As she saw two police cars pass in the street she absorbed the stuff that events are made of:

Mabel's birth, a bloody nose at three and the flu at five. Her first day at school, measles on graduation night, her tonsil operation, high school days, the first date with a boy she disliked, the morning she was caught inspecting her breasts, her last day at school, her strange eyes after hours on the roof with the man next door, her first job and the day she quit the job because her boss insisted upon dropping coins down her dress and then tried to fish for them, the night she hadn't come home and her violent answers to questions the next morning, the night she came home drunk and dripped love for a Mr. Jackson and his four children, the afternoon she came home with red hair, her new skirts exhibiting her knees, her new language, her new and bitter language, the telegram from Washington . . .

The ache of being caught in the custody of a panic made little chills spank her body.

Oh, dear Mabel, don't go away, don't go away. Please, Mabel, don't. I brought you up and don't go away. I took care of you and took care of you, never stopped taking care of you. Name me one day I haven't given you love. Name all the days I had the right to be cruel and hateful. I've been good to you. You know I've been good to you, and you know you haven't been good to me. You shout nasty things at me, and once you said something that made me cry for days. I remember this, Mabel. Some mothers might be glad that such daughters are leaving. I know some of those mothers. And, Mabel, I know some of those daughters. Sometimes I think I should be glad you're going away. Maybe life will be easier with you gone. But I'm lying to myself and life will be lonely without you. In spite of you, Mabel, I want you here. I want you here, here with me. When I married Harry, he wanted a boy and I prayed to God for a girl, and you came to live with us. It was a good life that day. People smiled and were nice and sweet and you were a little girl with blue eyes who was always asking why is this and why is that. And how I wanted you to stay that way forever. Oh, why did you have to grow up in this life that's wild and ugly with war? Why couldn't you remain small with your questions and your ribbons in your hair? And now the war is taking away Chesty, and you're going away next week to God-knows-where. Oh, Mabel, I can say more, you know I can say more, but you know what I've been trying to say. Oh, Mabel, I think I shall die if you go.

Mabel opened the door and shook a dose of salt into a pot of soup.

Mrs. Anderson said: Mabel, tell me, why, why can't you get work in New York?

Mabel said: I'll bite! Why?

Mrs. Anderson said: But it seems to me New York should have so many jobs.

Mabel said: Look, mother, look! Let's settle this thing once and for all! I can't find work here and I found work in Washington and I'm going to take that job! And if that isn't plain enough I shall print it on giant signs!

Mrs. Anderson said: But in Washington there's nothing but strangers. You'll be living alone. You never lived alone. You'll be unhappy. I'm your mother and I know you'll be unhappy alone.

God's in His heaven and all's wrong with Mrs. Anderson.

Mrs. Anderson said: This is your home, your place to live. Your family is here, and it's friendly here. You'll be losing something fine when you leave. Mabel, you'll be losing me, your mother.

Mabel contained perfect command of the answers to peel her mother's theory on the friendly home to its naked skin, but she persuaded herself to drop the issue and stir the soup.

It is better to have left you, mother dear, and lost, than not to have left at all.

Mrs. Anderson said: It will be a sad house with you gone.

Oh, God, is she kidding me? Can she really be serious? What makes her take these joy-rides? I've been snarling at her for so long a time that you'd think she'd hire a brass band and buy drinks for the city to see me off. Dear John Anthony, I have a problem for you, my mother by the window.

Mabel said: It would be an amazing idea if we set the table, you know. Pop and boys should be here soon.

Mrs. Anderson girdled her grief and paced through her duties as if it were a final encore to a part she had been playing too long in a vacant theatre, a part with worn and dry improvisations. She wanted to talk to Mabel, talk to her, reason with her and reason with her. There was so much to say, so much to say and go over, but there was no relative click between her tongue and brain. She sliced the bread.

Dear Mabel, I've suddenly become a very old woman. I'd like to tell you this, but I've told you so much, and if you don't understand that you won't understand this. Oh, why do I love you when I should hate you? I don't know why, oh, but I do know why. I know why I love you very much. I know why and I can tell you why, but it may not come out right. It's strange to think it may not come out right. It should be easy to talk to someone you love. Maybe I've become too old, old enough to be afraid you won't understand. I think that's it, dear Mabel. I think so very much.

She craved to hug her daughter and rub noses and hands as they did in the old days when she was young and her daughter was new, but the act seemed like some faded souvenir of a warm world that passed too quickly.

You can't have your Mabel and eat it.

The boom of Joe's voice banged through the hushed hallway,

and the severe voices of the old man and Chesty aided Joe in the removal of the silence. Mabel turned off the gas.

It's always fair weather when good fellows get together.

Skinny opened the door and reached for the bread.

CHAPTER 8

THE SUMMER wrath blistered the night, and Chesty left the restaurant with a dirty brown taste in his stomach. He thought it his civic duty to inquire of the Board of Health why some restaurants don't serve stomach pumps for dessert.

He hopped into a bumpy trolley car and wondered if his mother was enjoying the train ride to Washington, and as he picked meat from his teeth he wondered if Mabel missed her mother who was on her way to surprise her daughter. A man in a double-breasted suit was bellowing to a sweet young thing about his one helluva life with his ex-wife, and the trolley stopped at Lexington Avenue. Chesty stepped out.

A sign in front of a hotel read:

THE MANAGEMENT AND PERSONNEL

OF THE

JOHNSON MOTOR COMPANY

EXTEND GREETINGS TO THE ARMED FORCES,

MAIN BALLROOM.

Chesty stepped in.

Voices slurred through the big beige room, and every varnished inch of the floor was studded with khaki, men's suits and tasty dresses. A private was trying to feed black coffee to a technically liquored sergeant whose face was milk-white from one too many. A long bar zig-zagged its liquid trail to the end of the room, and there were photos of the war behind the bar. A marine on a swaying binge said to a girl with a shoebutton nose: this is Friday night, and for the life of me I can't help worrying who's helping my old man out of the Carson City Saloon, Nevada, U.S.A.

Chesty snake-hipped his way through a stack of bodies and watched the dancers from the bandstand. *One, two, one, two, three. One, two, one, two, three.* It looked so easy.

A trombonist was taking a hot solo. *Chinatown, my China-town, when the lights are low.* Chesty liked the choppy rhythm rocking out of the yellow slushpump, and he admired the trombonist's mustache. After the war he'd grow one for himself. And maybe he'd fiddle around with the trombone and play those choppy rhythms. Well, he'd see.

A manicured nail drilled into his back, and he turned to see two grey searchlight eyes flooding his face. He felt exposed.

Be nonchalant, keep cool, he thought. Smoke a butt. Smoke a few butts. But keep cool. *As it must come to all men, a Camel came to Chesty Anderson.*

She said: Hello, hello, sweet boy!

He said: Hello.

She said: My name's Linda. Observe my badge! I am a hostess for the night, and I've spent three hours here and, Lord, the place is truly beguiling! Dance?

He said: I don't know how.

She said: Well, sweet boy, nothing fazes Linda. We'll just sit you and Linda down and chat and chat.

She grabbed his arm and steered his body to a corner table. Someone plopped cokes before them, and she held her drink high, and he wondered what mental institution she escaped from.

She said: Whom shall we toast?

He said: Well, it seems to me we . . .

She said: To the King of England!

Chesty remembered one helluva tragic picture about old

France and a certain king who was having one helluva time of it, what with a shapely dame who didn't give a hang for him, she was nuts over a young guardsman, and his people who were pretty sore about being taxed for this and what-not. Well, the king was really having one helluva time of it. But the point was that there was a lot of drinking going on in the picture. Why, every minute or so the king's loyal dukes would spring to their feet, flutter their vaselined eyelashes and purr: to the king, gentlemen! Oh, those dukes certainly drank like hell through those seven reels, all right.

He said: To the King of England.

She said: I must confess that my secret pash is King George. He's so erect, every pound a king! But don't dare think I detest the queen! God, the way she smiles! God, the way she trails him! And their heavenly kids, Princess Elizabeth and Princess what's-her-name! The queen's sweet and he deserves her! And George, I mean the king, reminds me of Stanley Polanski. You've heard of the famous Polanski, I presume, all-American fullback, Notre Dame, 1942. In his revolting way, Stanley was a king. Lord, I was raving mad about the boy! But that vulture with the flirty eyes, Honey Dover, sunk her ugly claws into that dumb Polack, and now he's wedded to her, trapped like a rat! He's an ensign and she had that puss of hers lousing up the *Times:* Mr. and Mrs. L. Laurence Dover announce the marriage of their daughter, Honey, to Ensign Stanley Polanski. And there was Linda, me, holding the bag, carrying the torch, you might say!

Oh, but why should Linda perturb you, sweet boy, with woes of Linda. Tell itty witty Linda all about you. Tell Mata Hari when you're joining the Army, and don't you think Uncle Sam's Army deliciously wunderbar?

Oh, do tell Linda all about you, and you dasn't omit the torrid female who's to be your pin-up girl, and don't you think jeeps the cunningest contraptions? The other day I was minding my own business when a jeep's horn blew, and one of the darlingest creatures waved at me and I was thrilled to the core! He was the spittin' image of Stanley and George! And, sweet boy, please don't ask Linda where Linda found the guts, but the other me in me waved back and that wretched traffic just swallowed him! And there was poor Linda, me, with a shattered heart. Oh, say, that soldier boy was utterly divoon!

Tell me, are you passionate about the war? Linda is, and Linda is donating her all! Every man, woman and beast should donate their all! If I didn't, why, I'd feel like a Benedict Arnold!

I said to mother: Mother, Linda is joining up!

Mother said: What?

I said: Linda is joining the Waldorf Canteen, a hostess, me!

Mother said: Oh!

I said: Yes, mother, sacrifice is the word for Linda, me, and I'm inducting my all to slay the Hun!

I say to hell with Penny Vandergreer and Cissy De Cosmo! Let that dreadful upper clan rhumba with their officers! My aim is to pitch in with the American doughboy! Why, if I must say so, I've had beaucoup ensigns and captains! Yes, unrationed! One general was simply wacky over me, proposed to me every time he had me in the dark! But I say, give the officers back to the Vandergreers, the De Cosmos, those damn plundering Indians! Ours is not to ask why, ours is but to do and die! Yes, die!—if we must.

When the war began my body swelled with patriotism! Naturally, my weight remains 118, stripped! I was beholden to our chaps in uniform! And, sweet boy, Linda was—well, I'll be hung, swung and clubbed! That darlingest creature at the bar is the driver of that cunningest jeep! Why, he does look like Stanley and George, a blackhaired version! Oh, say, really, Linda is fraught and you must release nervous she! Linda must see that boy, get that boy, own that boy! Realize, realize Linda's plight! She must donate her all to the cause! Oh, sweet boy, it was perfectly thrilling talking to you! Our conversation was too enchanting! You are intensely interesting!

Really, really that! And when you're in precious uniform do, do come to the Waldorf Canteen and look up Linda, me! Having you would be just too adorable! Bye, bye!

Chesty nursed his coke and really, really thought of Stanley so-and-so and King George's heavenly kids, and he deeply wondered about that general who was simply wacky over Linda, me, and he wondered if he would be serving the best interests of mankind by offering condolences to that darlingest creature who drove that cunningest jeep, the black-haired version of—oh, hell, let's drop it!

Four score and seven years ago our fathers brought forth on this continent a new nation, conceived in liberty and dedicated to the proposition that all men are created for Linda what's-her-name.

He beelined across the ballroom and crushed his cigaret under the pastel banner of the Johnson Motor Company.

A sailor in the hotel lobby asked him if there were any beauts at the ball. Chesty said it was a convention for pigs, and the sailor thanked him very much and bounced out of sight. A stray out-of-town newspaper begged to be plucked, and he went next door to a cafeteria for coffee.

He thumbed through the paper and was amused over the social lions running amuck in the small town: Mrs. John Landin of Muncie, Indiana, is visiting the Clager Family. Craig London, new Rotarian chief. Miss Julia Arden to hold Bible classes at the Baptist Church. Jean Thal, of our town, is writing a book. Irma Hickey to lead the high school band. Send congratulations to Mrs. Ezra Rankin on her eighty-third birthday. A corner of the sporting page was consecrated to a mortician:

> We Are Proud To
> Offer Our Patrons
> The Choice Of One
> Of The Largest Stocks

Of Caskets In The
World. In Face Of
Shortages And Rising
Costs We Continue
To Offer Fine Funerals
At Lower Prices. How
Long We Can Do This
Is Problematical.
However, We Shall
Not Raise Our Prices
Until There Is No
Alternative.

Chesty wondered if Mrs. Ezra Rankin on her eighty-third birthday was taking full advantage of the ad, and he mulled over the idea of sending it to that utterly divoon hostess, c/o the Waldorf Canteen.

I got you on my list, you never will be missed.

He sipped his coffee and heard a man say it was raining cats and dogs outside. A busboy grinned and guessed it was okay for ducks and farmers. The man said something under his breath, and the busboy folded his grin. A Salvation Army major complained that her liverwurst was slightly green.

CHAPTER 9

THE SKY belched. The thunder of one more belch cracked the dark morning and the air became clogged with the twisting speed of the rain that beat the streets in a unified tempo of a thousand small drums.

Skinny walked slowly, slowly in the gutter. All of him, all of his possessions stuck out. The bones in his cheeks bulged like biles, and his nose was a shapeless hunk of beef, and his lips were full, and his ears were large, his chin long, his body bony and feeble, and his eyes were red with the cry for sleep, and his sleeveless shirt exposed arms like blunt sticks of chalk. He had a big head.

One more clap of thunder stuttered insanely, and Skinny scoffed at the scattering people on the mad hunt for shelter. Some huddled in doorways and some huddled under awnings and some made reluctant purchases for the franchise of being legitimate fugitives from the prison of the rain. Skinny and his big, wet head was a flawless model for a tragic cartoon as the people fled from the streets and he just wandered in the gutter while the rain spilled over and sucked his body.

He saw an organ grinder and a shaky old lady under an awning, and the organ grinder was tossing a long plea at his monkey dancing in the rain, and he looked at the lady and was sorry for her condition, and he released chivalry.

He said: Mrs., please, Mrs., please wear my organ cover. Please, Mrs.

The lady said: No, thank you very much. You are very kind. No.

Skinny sneered at the shaky lady. He watched the monkey and he liked the way the monkey clapped the rain between his purple hands, and he liked the way the monkey rejected the agony of his master to please, please come out of the rain, my little Zeeto. The monkey stopped his dancing and stared seriously at Skinny.

Skinny said: Hello, monkey.

The monkey held out his purple hands and Skinny wondered what purple hands felt like, and he heard the old lady say something about a foolish, such a foolish monkey, and he batted her with one more sneer, and he walked away and wondered very much if he had missed anything by not touching the purple hands.

When he reached the corner he turned around. The monkey kept staring at him as a simple child stares at a strange, complexed top. Skinny waved, and the monkey just stared while the hair of his tiny brown body soaked up the spleen of the rain. The organ grinder bombed the street with Italian curses, and the old lady shifted her legs and shut her eyes.

He said: Excuse me, Mrs. Don't hate me. But my monkey. Oh, my dumb monkey.

The lady said: Animals don't belong in civilized nations. Animals belong in Africa, only Africa.

Skinny turned the corner and shook his head. *That monkey and his purple hands. Jesus.*

Two girls ran past him as if the rain was discharging an evil disease. A woman swore and swore when a car splashed mud on her stockings, and her little girl fought bravely to crush a giggle.

Rain's wet, a man said to a fat friend. The friend laughed, and the man was encouraged to the point of pulling the ancient chestnut about what they do in Turkey when it rains. The friend doubled his output of laughter and the fat tubes of his belly wiggled over his belt. *Some joke for a couple of wise guys, but gimme Charlie Chaplin,* Skinny said.

A cop was standing under a newspaper shed. He yelled: Hey, kid, get outa the rain! *Break a leg, cop,* Skinny screamed in his big head. *Big, brave Mick with your dry blue uniform and gun and club.*

A Western Union boy raced past on a bike. A man was having a beer in the doorway of a bar.

A guy in a yellow raincoat was on the make for a knockout under a blue umbrella. *I'm the Sheik of Araby, my love belongs to thee.* The guy revealed his teeth and said something clever, and the girl murdered him in cold blood with a look that hadn't been washed for years, and she walked faster and he matched her stride for stride with his teeth revealed in the rain. *Fat chance, Mister Phony Baloney Yellow Raincoat,* Skinny said.

He passed an abandoned pushcart and snatched an apple. A peddler shouted from a doorway.

Skinny said: Come and get me!

His teeth tore through the apple. *Call this an apple? No juice!* The peddler shouted again and Skinny looked at the apple and looked at the peddler and threw the apple at the peddler, and it missed. A sailor and his girl laughed. The peddler looked at the laughing couple and relayed a rant. The girl quickly stopped her laughter and pinched the sailor to stop his. Skinny moved on. The sailor couldn't stop his laughter.

A few kids were playing Open Poker in a hallway. One of them looked out in the rain and saw Skinny in the gutter.

He said: Take a good look at that crazy Skinny!

His friends looked up and instinctively organized an off-key chorus for an emotional chant: Crazy, Skinny, crazy, crazy Skinny! Oh, you poor jerk of a crazy Skinny!

Skinny screamed that they should all take a flying one to the moon, no exceptions.

One kid said: Come in here and I'll tear your crazy head wide open!

A nervous violence racked Skinny: Inna rain I'll fight you! Bare fists inna rain! Slug it out like men inna rain!

The kids were stunned and the general opinion went around that Skinny lost his mind from too much rain.

One kid said: Hear that? Skinny wannsa fight Trigo, hard guy of P.S. 149!

Another said: They must be feeding Skinny dope at home!

Trigo's vanity was slit, and he had things to say to the dirty rain: wenna rain stops I'll kill Skinny once and for all!

One kid said: I make a motion that Skinny better pray the rain never stops!

Trigo said: I second the motion!

The kids went back to Open Poker. While fingering a card, Trigo said: Better take a fast trip to China, Skinny! America's too small for you and me!

Skinny sneered and looked up at the sky and the rain came

down thickly and his face and arms were wet and shiny, and he shook his fist at the sky and called Trigo a bitter name.

One kid said: Go home, your old lady wannsa feed you dope!

Another said: Skinny gotta big head fulla nothing! And his brother, Joe, gotta brain you can brag about! Figure that one out!

Trigo said: Someone oughta tell Joe I'm gonna kill his brother!

One kid said: Joe'll just hafta get along without a brother!

Trigo said: I second the motion!

For whom the Trigo tolls, it tolls for Skinny.

The fury in Skinny died a little and he retraced his steps. He passed the pushcart and snatched another apple, and the peddler shrieked, and Skinny heaved the apple at him, and it missed. The peddler looked at the sailor and his girl, and the sailor laughed, and his girl pinched him to flap his laughter, and the peddler picked up the apple and threw it at Skinny, and it missed. The sailor grew abnormal with laughter, and the peddler's eyes sizzled and he advanced toward the sailor, and the girl promptly asked him for a pound of apples, and the peddler opened his eyes widely and smiled very nicely. The sailor couldn't stop his laughter.

These people, Skinny said. *They race like wild dogs inna street. They hide in doorways and watch the rain from safe places. They buy things they don't need. Look at them buying things they don't need. Look at them watch the sky and wanna know why it hadda rain today. Wottsamatta? Afraid of rain? Think the rain'll ruin you? Ruin's just a lotta water! Wottaya got against water? And me, just a kid, Skinny and no meat and no muscles! And I walk slow inna gutter! And I say up and in you to the rain! And I say you people ain't got guts and I got guts and I'll fight you inna rain if you say I ain't got guts! And I spit at the rain!* And he spit at the rain.

He saw the cop reading a newspaper. *Nothing to do but read, cop. Get on your beat! Walk around! Maybe a man's choking his wife down the block! Arrest that man!*

He saw the beerdrinker with an empty glass in the doorway of the bar. *Fill your glass, you cheap bum!*

He saw the fat man and his friend, and the friend was silent and the fat man wasn't laughing. *Wottsamatta, Mister, outa jokes for your big fat balloon of a friend? Go and see Charlie Chaplin, Fatty!*

He saw the woman and her child under a shed, and the woman was wiping mud from her stockings, and the child who was giggling was now crying. *Wottayawanna make the kid cry for? Talk to kids! Talk to kids! Don't hit kids! Oh, Jesus, you're one helluva mother!*

He turned the corner and saw the organ grinder hug the monkey like mothers hug babies, and he heard the monkey squeal like a baby, and he heard the organ grinder blubber like a mother to hush the monkey, his baby. He sneered at the monkey and thought his purple hands very ugly.

He saw the shaky old lady wearing the organ cover around her shoulders, and her posture was being constantly broken by her shivering, and she was tapping her feet to destroy the shiver and recapture her dignity. She called out to Skinny: If you don't get out of the rain, young man, you will catch your death of cold, your very death of cold!

Skinny stuck his tongue between his lips and produced a Bronx Cheer.

The lady said: Why, you dirty, dirty little thing!

Skinny produced one more cheer and walked down the street and stopped before a store window and saw his image through the glass. He saw the rain roll from his big head to his shapeless hunk of nose, and he wiped the rain that dripped from his nose, and he waved at his image, and his image waved back limply, and he lifted his lips and tried to smile, and his teeth seemed to hang and sway from his gums, and he remembered the night his brother, Joe, said that he looked like a goddamn wet skeleton after taking a bath, and he felt that he was going through a bath, and he tried to forget and to never, never remember what Joe said he looked like. He walked away from his image very slowly, very slowly and very sadly. *This is my own, my native image.*

Something new had been added to the rain, lightning.

CHAPTER 10

THE WINDOW was closed and the shade was down and the bedroom was smelly and sticky with the red heat of July, and three flies and a roach were strolling along the wall.

Joe got up. He dressed slowly and walked slowly into the bathroom and washed and walked slowly back to the bedroom and pulled up the shade and said: Goddamn! The flies flew from the wall and gummed their bellies to the window. The roach continued his stroll. It was raining.

Joe looked into the mirror and mechanically combed his hair the way his father combed his hair and the way his two brothers combed their hair—the same part on the side, the same hereditary slew of curls, the same strands falling over the eye, the same, the same, day in the same, day out the same. But someday he would pompadour his hair. All the way up and no goddamn part! *That's a goddamn day I can't wait for!*

He went into the kitchen and felt hemmed in by a sloppy floor and a dampness snarling from the walls and ceiling. He looked around for the bread and butter. A bottle of milk sat alone on the table, ashamed in its solitude.

Where's the goddamn bread and where's the goddamn butter? Oh, goddamn this and goddamn that and why in goddamn did Mom hafta go to Washington? And why in goddamn don't Pop leave me some dough? What does he goddamn think I'm gonna live on, my goddamn looks? And where the goddamn is Skinny? Oh, goddamn it all! No bread, no butter! Just milk, milk, white medicine! A goddamn bottle of white medicine! Thank you, Mr. Borden, very much! With your stuff in me I'll be another Dempsey! Yeah!

From the street came the staccato bark of a dog and a woman's shrill voice. Joe curiously opened the window. The rain was letting up. A woman with a stiff, angry mouth was shaking a finger at a husky airedale: Why, why do you do this to me? Don't I feed you at home? Don't I buy you the best money can afford? Can you show me one dog, one dog as well-fed as you? Why in God's name must you poke your nose in garbage cans? Why? Why?

The dog simply turned from her and ambled over to sniff at a bulging garbage can, and the woman's face blew up into a color spasm of pink and blue. She raged: All right, Brownie, if that's the way you want it! Now you are on your own! Do you hear? Now you are on your own! I'm through with you! We're washed up! Through, once and for all! Understand me, Brownie? Through for good, you hear? I should worry, I should care what happens to you! Goodbye and good luck!

The dog nonchalantly selected and nibbled at a compound of garbage that dangled invitingly from the can. The woman dug her shoes into the pavement and dashed off, her pink and blue face stuck high in the air and washed by the rain.

Goddamn woman and her goddamn dog!

Joe shut the window and opened the icebox and the pantry and the drawer under the table. *Ain't this one helluva goddamn naked kitchen! Old Mother Hubbard went to her cupboard, and you can take it from there!*

The door opened and Skinny came in, every space of him drenched.

Joe said: Where the goddamn were you?

Skinny said: Taking a walk.

Joe said: Inna rain?

Skinny said: I'm not afraid of rain.

Joe said: Do me a favor and run like hell to Bellevue and get that goddamn head of yours looked over!

Skinny felt his flesh tumbling like an acrobat, and he sat on the window ledge for a prop, his eyes broody and hurt and pinned tightly to Joe.

Joe said: Where's the bread and butter?

Skinny said: Search me.

Joe said: Did you have any?

Skinny said: I didn't eat.

Joe said: I'm starved!

Skinny said: Maybe Pop finished it.

Joe said: Did he leave any money?

Skinny said: Not for me.

Joe said: For Chesty?

Skinny said: Search me.

Joe said: Everything for Chesty! Goddamn everything for smart guy Chesty who knows alla big words by their first name! He quits a job three weeks ago to wait for the Army to grab him and now he doesn't do nothing but read books and take walks! I need a vacation, he says to Pop! So he gets a vacation! A goddamn vacation with books and walks!

Skinny said: We'll eat okay when Mom gets back.

Joe said: And take Mom? Did she hafta go and see that goddamn stinker of a Mabel? Did she hafta leave us inna cold with an old man who can't see nothing but Chesty's this and Chesty's that and Chesty's goddamn muscles?

Skinny said: Search me.

Joe said: Search me, search me! Goddamn, say something with guts, you goddamn skinny little punk!

Everything in Skinny seemed to droop. He turned his face and his lips shook and his nose left an imprint on the window, and then he felt the arrival of a fat anger fry inside of him, and he felt the anger hiss in his chest and tighten his throat, but the anger was locked up inside of him and it wouldn't come out, and his eyes smoked from the anger that wouldn't come out.

Joe watched his brother's drawn, glum face, and he didn't feel sorry for hurting him, and he didn't want to say he was sorry, even if by just saying he was sorry and not meaning it would decrease the pain he had caused. His mind was occupied by a mean little gladness leaping crazily in his head for hurting him, and the gladness made him warm, and he thanked the mean little gladness for the warmth that made him feel so goddamn good.

He said: See the guys?

Skinny despised his voice that bounced back lamely from the window: They're playing Open Poker on Sixth Street.

Joe mouthed the milk bottle and thought of the great day he'd drink nothing but beer for breakfast. He gargled the stuff cows give and left the house, and Skinny left the window ledge and emptied the milk down his throat. The rain stopped.

Joe walked down the street. He saw the woman and her dog. The dog was licking her fingers while the woman laughed like a happy, harmless moron. She rubbed her painted face into the dog's face and sank her fingers into his neck, and the melting ooze of her voice made Joe wish he had a gun: My darling! My great big, great big darling and his great big appetite. How can I be mad at my darling? But, Brownie, you must promise me right this very minute that you won't eat any more garbage! I insist upon that! Yes, darling, yes, no more garbage from now on. Now, darling is coming home with me to see what a special surprise I bought for him, just for him. Oh, won't he be delighted!

Skinny saw Joe from the window, and he saw a woman and her dog acting in the great tradition of devoted lovers, and now he was alone and the anger was coming out of him as if it were something human, something wild and alive, and the heat of his words made abstract designs on the window pane: Hungry, Joe? Starved, Joe? Well, go out and steal! You're old enough, Joe! And goddamn you, Joe, you lousy punk, you lousy goddamn punk with your strong shoulders and strong arms and strong legs! Goddamn you for making me feel like I feel! But I'll tell you this, Joe! Someday I ain't gonna be the sick little cripple you think I am! Can you hear me, Joe? Goddamn you, Joe, can you hear me, can you hear me? I'm not talking to you, Joe! I'm yelling at you, Joe! Can you hear me? Can you hear me say that someday, Joe, someday!

He saw Joe cross the street, and the fury of the rain came down again to swamp the streets, and the woman and her dog hailed a taxi, and Joe ducked under an awning, and Skinny's lips grew full with bubbles of saliva, and fresh designs covered the window pane: Afraid of rain, Joe? Why, you're nothing but a lousy yellow goddamn lousy yellow goddamn punk! And that's all, Joe! That's all!

He turned from the window and killed a roach that was creeping from the bedroom.

CHAPTER 11

ERNIE, PLEASE keep your shirt on and please listen to me. Please, Ernie . . . But how can I talk louder when she's in the next room? . . . Oh, Ernie you know how much I want to see you. Is it so hard to understand that, darling? And what pleasure do you get out of driving me crazy? . . . But it will be only for a few days and then she'll be gone, thank God. . . . Oh, how many times must I tell you that I didn't invite her, I didn't want her. I can do without her, Ernie. . . . But she's here and what can I do, and why did she have to come and make you so angry and me so miserable? . . . Ernie, you know good and darn well how much I love you, and how I'll be living in hell until she gets out of here and stays out. And you know all this, Ernie, every little bit of it and still you torture me and torture me, and, darling, I ask you to please, please stop it. . . . Yes, I hid your clothes, she'll never know. . . . Yes, yes, I took care of everything. I didn't miss a trick. I even hid that picture of your ugly wife. . . . Of course I'm jealous. I'm green with the stuff, and I feed my jealousy with a tablespoon of your wife's face every night. . . . Oh, darling, I must hang up. Please understand why. . . . Yes, I'll try hard to get rid of her just as soon as I can. . . . Goodbye, Ernie. Be good, be careful, think of me living in hell until you come back, and, Ernie, take care of that cold of yours. . . . Ernie, kiss me. Of course I'll feel it. . . . Yes, I know why a kiss over the phone is like a straw hat. . . . Oh, darling, I'll miss you so much tonight. . . . Yes, I know you're working tomorrow. I'll call you at your office in the morning. . . . Yes, I'll call you the moment she leaves. I won't waste a second. You can depend on that, and you can take odds on that . . . I love you, Ernie.

She walked across the foyer of her apartment, puffs of wrath shooting in and out of her nose. The skinny frame of a woman sitting lifelessly in a chair reminded her of Whistler's Mother, and she felt like a cat in the act of destroying a mouse as she stole up to her mother.

She said: Don't tell me you're tired!

Her mother said: Mabel, you scared me! Yes, I'm tired. The train was so crowded. So much talking, so much smoking. One poor lady fainted. Mabel, you scared me, you know that.

Mabel said: Trains aren't cemeteries, you know. And did I really scare poor, sweet mother? Oh, I'm so very sorry!

Her mother said: Mabel . . .

Mabel said: Couldn't you wire me you were coming? Or send a letter? Must you surprise me this way? Must you present yourself as if you were a special delivery package?

Her mother said: Mabel, what a terrible thing to say to mother.

Mabel said: I hate surprise visits! It's like being caught with your pants down!

Her mother said: Your language, Mabel.

Mabel said: Oh, cut it out!

Her mother said: Am I in your way, dearest? Don't you want

me?

Mabel said: I said cut it out!

Her mother said: Mabel, there's something wrong with you and you must tell mother what's wrong. I insist, Mabel.

Mabel said: Mother, please cut it out! . . . Who's caring for Pop and the boys?

Her mother said: Milk will be delivered every morning. Father will leave them enough money to eat out.

Mabel said: How's Pop?

Her mother said: Working so hard.

Mabel said: And the boys?

Her mother said: I'm worried about Joe. He's so bitter. Chesty left the Johnson Motor Company a few weeks ago. He wants a vacation before he's drafted.

Mabel said: He hated that job. You'll never know how much he hated it. I'm so sure you'll never know.

Her mother said: For father's sake I'm glad he never took that job with that publishing house. Father would have been so hurt. He's so proud of Chesty coming home dirty and strong from work. And the way he watches Chesty eat!

Mabel said: How's Skinny?

Her mother said: Mabel, must you call him that? My poor baby. He's always alone and feeling out of place.

Mabel said: What about you?

Her mother said: I still get the same pains. Sometimes it's hard to bear.

Mabel said: When are you going home?

Her mother said: Mabel, something is terribly wrong with you. And you have no right at all to hold it from your mother who has loved you and protected you, clothed you, fed you and who hasn't stopped crying since the day you left home to come here and live alone. And if nothing is wrong then why haven't you written in four months? Four months, four long months, and no word from my daughter in four months. And that is exactly why I'm here, Mabel. I'm going to find out things and take care of you as I've done. Exactly.

Mabel said: Oh, there you go again and here I go again to tell you to cut it out! And you can do me a great, personal favor by not coming here again! I repeat: you can do me a great, personal favor by not coming here again!

Her mother's body heaved and then sagged in her chair, and she stared dumbly at the floor and Mabel thought of a slab of sick, shriveled meat, and she wanted to scream and grow vile and pro-fane and drive the sick meat from her apartment with a stream of humiliating curses, but she picked up a magazine and tried to read and she couldn't locate the continuity of the words, and she looked at her mother and again the thought of sick meat disfigured her imagination, and she was sure that all this was a scientific plot to quickly entomb her within the walls of the insane.

Oh, why did this skinny woman have to come here and force Ernie to leave? And why isn't stupidity considered a major crime, and why isn't my mother jailed for not knowing that home was a daily hell of obedience, and now I'm free, and now I hate her, and I hated the way she washed me and combed me and fed me and clothed me and caged me as if I were a rare blue-ribbon pet, thoroughbred stock, terrific pedigree. And now Ernie will be missing tonight, and I got the mad-about-him, sad-about-him, how can I be glad-without-him blues. And tonight's Saturday night, the technicolor night of the week, and some think this night is made for fun and frolic and so do I, and oh how I miss you tonight, Ernie, and oh how I hate you, you stupid, skinny, stupid woman for not knowing how much I hate you.

Her mother rose from her chair and patiently patted Mabel's hair.

Forgive them, for they know not what they are doing.

She said: What's the matter, dear Mabel? Tell mother whats the matter.

Mabel said: Oh, nothing's the matter! No, nothing!

She said: Don't you like Washington?

Mabel said: I love Washington madly!

She said: Are you unhappy here?

Mabel said: I am tremendously happy here!

She said: Have you met any nice people?

Mabel said: Some of my best friends are nice people!

She said: Perhaps it's your job?

Mabel said: My job fascinates me!

She said: And your health? It may be your health you know.

Mabel said: I'll match my health against any corpse you select!

She said: Mabel, how sharp your tongue is.

Mabel said: The better to snarl at you, mother dear! And I warn you not to ask what big teeth I have!

She said: Mabel, what has Washington done to you? Hadn't you better come home with me?

Mabel said: Washington hasn't made me that much of an idiot to want to go home with you!

She said: Dearest Mabel, you can tell me what's the matter with you.

Mabel crushed her red nails into the magazine, and her voice was just a feeble reproduction of the violent voice slamming within her.

She said: Can I? Oh, say, that's decent of you!

Her mother said: Maybe you need sleep, a good, old fashioned sleep. Try that, Mabel. Listen to mother.

Mabel's irritation reached a raw, blistering height. It was as if the irritation was spluttering in her throat and lynching her with a specially designed rope. She shot from her chair and ran to the bathroom, banged the door and leaned against the sink and cried. Her mother gently tapped on the door and asked what in the wide world was the matter and if she could please be of any help, please Mabel.

Mabel said: Leave me alone! Will you leave me alone?

Her mother said: If you should need me, poor girl, call me.

Mabel looked into the mirror and her face made her think of the night Ernie had told her he was married, and how she had raced out of bed and cried in the bathroom. Yes, the same bloodless face and the same snapping lines around the mouth. She dried her tears and walked out of the bathroom. She said it would be a good idea if they went to a movie. Her calmness astonished her. She felt that congratulations were in order.

Her mother said: No, dear, you go. I feel my pains coming on.

Mabel was conscious of tiny thrills of joy over the pains her mother felt coming on. *Oh, they should come more often, mother dear.*

She powdered her face and said she'd be back at eleven, and that her mother shouldn't wait up for her. She walked down the street and thought of her more penetrating intimacy with the darkness than with her mother, and at the end of the street a movie marquee tattooed the darkness with neon.

After the movie she went to an ice cream parlor and had a soda, and she thought of how her mother would love some ice cream, and how her mother would be delighted over her gesture, but the thought of buying anything to please her mother was sour and alien. She walked out of the ice cream parlor without ice cream.

She passed Helen Arbuckle, who worked with her in the War Department, and she said hello to Helen, who was holding the hand of a blond man, and as she walked home she thought of Ernie and his rough hands and felt his face burning in the darkness, and a loneliness weakened her, and she realized what a frail, sensitive instrument the human mind can be.

I got a right to sing the blues . . . my mother is in bed where Ernie should be.

She opened the door silently, clicked the foyer light and undressed. She climbed into bed very noiselessly and repulsively drew away from the icy contact of her mother's legs, and she wondered where in Washington would Ernie be sleeping tonight, and the pain for him came again, and she cried again, and she soaked her face into her pillow in fear of her mother hearing her cry, and the horror of one more question forced her into deliriums of grotesque apparitions that resembled gigantic telephones and gigantic voices bellowing, Ernie, I love you, Ernie, I love you, Ernie, I love you, and then came the sharp switch to gigantic tears flooding bloody bathrooms and a gigantic stadium filled with millions of skinny women, and all the skinny women looked like her mother, and all the skinny women were cackling and conspiring to seduce her discovery of freedom, Ernie and Washington with questions, questions, questions, millions and millions of questions, millions of questions gliding from gigantic lips. *Oh, mother, my life a hell you're making.*

The sun in the morning snapped her sleep and her mother's deep sleep annoyed her. She slipped into a robe, entered the kitchen and winced when she pressed a wet cloth to her head to reduce the roar of an ache.

She prepared coffee and went to her mother and tapped her shoulder, and her mother didn't move. She tapped her again, and when no response came she pushed her, and her mother didn't move. She received a quick impulse to write a note: *Phone call came. Must report for work. See you tonight.* Ingenious idea! Masterpiece of strategy! Eight hours of banished agony!

But the deep sleep was provoking and the coffee was getting cold, and she pinched her mother's arm, and when that didn't help she yanked the pillow from her mother's head, and that didn't help.

Then she recalled the pains. She calmly telephoned the doctor who lived next door. She returned to her mother and pinched her face and slapped her face and called her name loudly and very loudly, and called her other things very loudly, and her mother didn't move. She went to the kitchen, sipped coffee and waited for the doctor.

The doctor came and examined Mrs. Anderson while Mabel was filing her nails. He questioned Mabel. He asked what time had she left her mother the night before. Mabel said it was around eight. The doctor looked at his watch and said it was now around nine, and that her mother was dead, a heart attack. She had been dead for approximately twelve hours . . . *twelve hours* . . . *weep no more, my lady, oh, weep no more today.*

The starkness of sleeping with a dead woman all night long, feeling dead legs, pinching a dead face, slapping a dead face, calling a dead woman's name, calling a dead woman names caused a rawness to blanket her scalp, and caused ugly little pimples to spring from her arms, and oh how she longed for the ability to produce a racking sob for the doctor's benefit, but the sob, the sincerity of the sob was something distant and unrelated to her. If only she were able to produce a reasonable facsimile, a white mournful face. But no, diplomacy was not one of her emblems. She felt cheated of dramatic talent. She asked the doctor what to do.

The doctor said she should try not to worry, death is death, and it's too bad it has to happen, but it comes to everyone. Mabel asked if the body can be removed before the evening, and the doctor said: yes.

Mabel emphasized that the body must, must be removed before the evening, and the doctor nodded and said he'd take care of it and that she shouldn't worry and that he'd send her his bill. Mabel walked him to the door, thanked him very much for his services and wondered why those pimples, those damn pimples remained stuck to her arms.

And then came the thought of having to go home, the thought of having to inform her father and her brothers about her mother's death, and the weary thought of going back to New York made her fret and regard the inevitable act as excess baggage.

She sat down and filed her thumbnail and looked at her mother dead in bed and wondered how Whistler's Mother would look dead in bed, and then the many precisely developed photos of her life with her mother flashed through her mind in a rapid parade of retrospect, and she was able to sense the crumbling, the actual crumbling and final dust of the black closet that confined her to the suction of her mother's mind. And now the past was amputated, amen. And the rut of a hollow cavity remained as a rude memento to forget, amen. And Mabel wanted to sing and sing songs of celebration. And she thought of Ernie, amen. And she put away her nail file and raced to the phone and hurriedly dialed the number of his office.

Ernie, oh, my darling, my strong piece of man, I have wonderful news for you! You can come back tonight! Do you hear, you can come back tonight? Everything is all right!

CHAPTER 12

THE WALLS of the room were thin and the gloomy insinuation of a trumpet playing the blues wailed from the flat next door, and they were sitting around the room and no one spoke, and the old man hated the trumpet and its requiem that was blotting out a broken narrative of things past while his eyes were pasted to Chesty's face, lifeline to his youth.

Skinny watched his father, and so did Joe, and Skinny felt like the dirty end of a stick, and Joe was the sulky bull resenting the hard stare of his father at a favorite son. Mabel was smoking a cigaret and thinking of the Fourteenth Street Car rumbling past the White House and the State Department and up Constitution Avenue to stop at the War Department, and she thought of her work on the third floor of the Department: filing systems, big green cabinets, blue cards, salmon cards, white cards, cards, cards, cards. *Miss Anderson, please look up 3483010. Miss Anderson, please look up the birth of so and so. Miss Anderson, these cards are to be put in alphabetical order. Miss Anderson, these cards are to be put in numerical order. Miss Anderson, Miss Anderson, Miss . . .* And she thought of Ernie.

The old man said: Look at me now and you wouldn't think that I once lifted a piano. And do you know something, Chesty? I think you can lift a piano.

Chesty said: Joke number one: there's a law against lifting pianos. Joke number two: pianos can be lifted by fools like me, but only Steinway can make a piano.

Joe said: A goddamn piano ain't tin, Pop, and don't forget it.

The old man said: If I did it, Chesty can do it.

Chesty said: But did you play it at the same time? Do that and it would make you the greatest opening act in American vaudeville.

The old man said: Again I say that you can lift a piano.

Chesty said: Pop, do me a favor and change your brand of cigarets.

The old man shrunk from the jab of the wisecrack. He then quivered with the crazy fever that always came to him and came to him, a fever that punched through his body and injected him with the hot urge to rise and rip the clothes from Chesty's body, to caress his muscles, to jam his fingers into his spine and dart his hands over the smooth swell of his chest, to pet the shape of his legs, but the quick fear of his children's failure to understand his act of tribute to the glory of the exposed body caused the shuttering of his eyes and the permit of his mind to sprint into the safety of his mental attic that he had established as an escape, and where he had stored a fund of imagery, an album containing the soiled portraits of young Harry Anderson lifting wagons and trunks to the amazement of his friends. They called him the strong boy of East St. Louis. They drank beer to toast his strength. And then, oh, the spicy relish of his lifting a piano one summer night, the crowning achievements of young Harry Anderson, the triumph of brawn, the body lined with the crisp bulge of meat. They gave him a girl that night. It was his friend's contribution to please the young king. And what a pretty dish to set before the king! *Taxation without representation.*

And now my body is rotten, old, and you, Chesty, you're my first son, my strength, and I swear to God that without strength a man's a sick cat in a cellar. And, Chesty, I gave you the strength. Remember that. I gave you the strength to use, to never lose. And, Chesty, Chesty, remember this and remember this and nail it to your head: don't be a sick cat like your old man. Beads of neck sweat crumpled the starch of his collar.

The blues of the trumpet rose to a growl and a loneliness slid into Skinny and he wanted the trumpet to stop, please stop. Chesty muttered something about writing to his Congressman regarding the playing of sad trumpets. Skinny swore that the blues forced the walls to shiver, and then the blues reached its last bar and died softly. Mabel killed her cigaret.

It was Sunday afternoon and the family had spent the morning in a cemetery where they heard a priest mumble in Latin and wave a cross while the old man placed white flowers on a mound of granulated dirt. *The hand that rocked the cradle was dead.*

At a nearby grave two girls and a lady in black were hysterical, and the communication of their lament became a bond, and Chesty and Joe wept, and Skinny gripped the inside of his cheeks to halt the burst of a cry, and Mabel was attracted by the shapely legs of the lady in black, and the old man tasted the salt of his tears and wondered what was going to happen to a home without a mother to cook and clean and go to bed with. The priest kissed the cross.

They were silent on the train back home. They filed into the house, a diagram of sick hearts, one for each other. Skinny picked up a telegram that was under the door. It was a message of sorrow from an aunt in Buffalo, and the old man read it in a low voice. Then Joe pointed to a hat on a hook and Chesty said it was Ma's, and he and his brothers sat down, their bodies shot and creased, and the old man stared at Chesty and hated the trumpet that blotted his youth, and Skinny and Joe took sensitive stock of their father's stare; and Mabel smoked and thought of the Fourteenth Street Car rumbling past the White House and the State Department and up Constitution Avenue to stop at the War Department, and she thought of Ernie.

The afternoon turned to bluegrey, and Joe came out of the kitchen and said: It's getting dark and when and where the goddamn are we gonna eat? I'm starved!

The old man shook his head and desperately tried to grasp a program, a firm set of rules and regulations to govern the house now that his wife was gone. *Baby, won't you please come home.* He had asked Mabel to stay home and replace her mother, but Mabel's answer was an eloquent yawn, and the old man tried and tried to think of a program, but no program took shape, and he felt utterly spent, a battered old man in a mission singing hymns for soup and bread.

Oh, God, wottahell am I gonna do when I don't make enough money for kids to eat in restaurants? And kids shouldn't eat in restaurants! Restaurants are okay for guys with white collars and change for tips, but kids must eat in kitchens! But who the damn is gonna cook for our kitchen? Oh, God, what shall become of us?

He said: Well, I guess we'll just hafta eat at the Automat again.

Chesty said: I'm not hungry.

Joe said: The hell with you! I'm starved!

Chesty said: Shut your trap, Joe!

Joe said: Aw, save your goddamn fighting for the Army!

Chesty said: Introducing my loud brother.

The old man said: Is this a day to fight?

Mabel said: What a house to live in!

Joe said: Go back to Washington! Who asked for you inna first place! You're no goddamn bargain!

Mabel said: You're a nasty dog, Joe!

Joe said: You're a nasty dog, Joe! Go screw!

Chesty said: There goes that dirty mouth!

The old man said: Better watch out, Joe. Chesty's like a lion. He'll kill you.

Joe said: But when do we goddamn eat?

Chesty said: Pop, your son is starving.

The old man handed Joe a dollar and told him to take Skinny with him, and Skinny's eyes snapped like lit matches: No one hasta take me anyplace, Pop, anyplace!

Joe said: Will you listen to the goddamn skinny punk?

Chesty said: Your dirty mouth should win prizes!

The old man said: Better go, Joe. Don't get killed.

Joe said: I live here! He knows what he can do!

Chesty said: Get the hell out of this room!

The old man said: Better go, Joe.

Joe said: Pop, don't be his goddamn stooge. Get wise!

Chesty lunged for Joe and the old man smiled, but Joe was fast and darted from the room, and Skinny followed him slowly and sneered at him for running away from anyone, anyone. Mabel said it was a horrible house and that she was going to catch the 7:20 for Washington.

The old man said: Mabel, please stay home. What are we gonna do?

Mabel said: Chesty will be in the Army. You'll be able to take care of Joe and Skinny.

The old man said: But wottsa house without a woman? A house is a hole without a woman.

Mabel said: I'm in no mood to grow old over a stove.

Chesty said: Go back to Washington, Mabel. Walk along the Potomac and dream of Coolidge with the light brown hair.

The old man said: But a house needs a woman, Chesty.

Mabel said: Find a wife. Don't waste your life in a cold bed.

The old man said: I'm an old man. You're not talking to Chesty. Look at him. He's strong. Now look at me. Who'd wanna old man?

Chesty said: Now look at Mabel, Pop. Three days here and she'd blow her brain.

The old man said: But what's so hot in Washington?

Mabel said: The Daughters of the American Revolution!

The old man said: Stay home, Mabel. Please, Mabel. Do it for your old man.

Chesty said: Pop, lay off, will you? She's strictly from Washington!

The old man said: Whatever you say, Chesty, whatever you say. All my life I've lived on ropes and ladders and ropes and ladders. Never sure of myself, always drifting, always swinging in the air. Now your mother is gone and I have Skinny, I have Joe, and I have you, Mabel. But, Chesty, you're the one I want, the one I need. You're my youth in East St. Louis, my strong boy, my answer to those who kicked me around when my strength died. You're my first son, Chesty, and you'll be leaving for the Army in twelve days and maybe you'll die in the Army, and maybe you'll come marching home. But if you die, I'll die. If you come marching home, I'll come marching with you. I'm in you, Chesty. I hangout in your body. Wherever you go, whatever you do, whatever happens . . . well, Chesty, I'll be along, me, your old man, always in your body, my body, strong as a lion, a king, you and me knocking homeruns, making touchdowns, you and me, Chesty, setting the world on fire, father and son, Harry and Chesty Anderson.

Chesty said: Is that your manifesto, Harry Anderson?

The old man said: Is this a time for jokes when you'll be leaving in twelve days? I told you all this before, but I gotta tell it to you again because you're leaving in twelve days and I wanna see that you don't forget it.

Thirty days hath September, April, June and November, all the rest have thirty-one, except Chesty, he has twelve.

Mabel keenly watched the performance before her. She sensed the ease in which she was able to insert herself into her brother and her mother into her father, and her breath flowed tensely and it regulated the rapid rise and fall of her breasts, and she remembered the drama of making coffee for a dead woman seven days ago, and it seemed that she had been sitting in her chair for seven long days, and she looked around and felt the confusion of the room crowding her and a stuffiness choking her, and when her head spurted dizzily she knew she had to leave at once. *You take the high road and I'll take the low road, and I'll be in Washington before you.* She powdered her face, briskly kissed her father, wished her brother luck in the Army, said she'd write and left the house.

The old man said: Now we're alone, you and me, alone.

Chesty nodded and closed his eyes tiredly and opened his eyes and walked to the window. He saw a Negro boy talking to a white girl and a Negro boy. He saw his sister walk past them, turn to look at them, walk on and turn to look at them again, continue walking, reach the corner, turn once more to look at them, walk around the corner and out of sight. The two Negro boys shook the hand of the white girl and parted. *We hold these truths to be self-evident.*

The old man observed his son with the adoration of a lover. The strength in his son's body delighted him, and the passion for his son's muscles to dance in and out furnished a sensuous lust to thrive in his now warm and cozy body. He thought of his son in the Army, a tough structure wrapped in khaki. God, he'd show him off! He'd buy a camera and take pictures of him in uniform, and he'd take pictures of him lifting a piano, and he'd mail the pictures to those he knew in East St. Louis, and, by God, he'd show them! Yes, he'd show them in East St. Louis, all right! You're damn right!

This boy is my boy, Chesty, son of Harry Anderson, proof of my strength!

The dazzling sequence made the old man sleep, and his youth came back to him in vivid flesh tones. Chesty saw his father asleep.

He reached into his pocket, counted eighty-seven cents, thought of the Automat, hoped that Joe wouldn't be there, silently moved around the room, changed his shirt, ran water over his hair and combed it, touched his mother's hat, opened the door, shut it lightly, lit a cigaret, walked down the stairs and his feet thumped against the wood.

Blab, blab, blab. Charles Atlas, Tarzan of Manhattan, the Body Beautiful, Sampson, thy name is Chesty Anderson. Blab, blab, blab. Lifting pianos to thrill the natives this side and that side of the Volga. Dumb guys with physical culture muscles. Burly bodies and dusty brains. Superior asses with superior asses. Muscles in the chest and muscles in the legs and muscles in the arms and muscles in the head. Muscles to the right of you and muscles to the left of you, and what the hell does it get you—varicose veins! Blab, blab blab.

The trumpet from the flat next door blared. This time the tune was hot and bubbly.

CHAPTER 13

THEY LEFT the Roxy and the moon was diluting the scorch of the sun and they walked along sweating and laughing, and Chesty couldn't expel the stage show's Cuban dancer with the purple tights who had raised hell with his temperature. *The very thought of you—Miss Purple Tights.*

A clinging soldier and his clinging girl friend passed them, and Chuck slapped Chesty's back and said: The Army's okay! Don't forget it! You get dames, good grub, goddamn good clothes, goddamn good things! You march in parades and the people cheer and the mayor makes a speech: It's the life of Reilly! An imported French General kisses your cheeks, ooh, lah, lah! A writer makes you a character in his book! You get free Pepsi-Cola and the beauties from the movies give you free passes to their lips! You're a front-page hero on a big job to murder fascism! But one thing's wrong, Chesty. One bastard thing. You might wind up dead. Stinking, stinking dead.

They piled into a bar.

Chesty despised the smell of a bar. Booze, beer, gin made his insides riot and lose its grip and grow sloppy, and then lumps of foam would swim in his stomach and he'd vomit.

They asked him what he'd have. He scratched his teeth. He said he'd have a beer. They said he was going to be a soldier and a soldier was a man and men drink scotch. They ordered scotch. He smiled and said that beer was his favorite drink, nothing like a glass of beer, nothing. The bartender drew it.

A terrible fear disorganized him as he watched the brown liquid rush into a glass and form a white head. His mind became active with the disturbing vision of being wheeled away in an oxygen tent, and then a surgeon to knife him apart and drain his beer. He glanced around for the men's room. He saw a sign under a blue bulb. The beer was before him and looked up at him. He sighed very heavily. He kept his eye on the sign.

They were out for one helluva good time, and they said it was their patriotic duty to give Chesty a real American send-off. One of them said he'd get so stewed, so cockeyed that they'd have to ship him home parcel post.

Another said: Chesty, if I should get drunk and start yelping about Sweet Adeline will you please slit my throat, please?

Chesty said he would, gladly.

They drank their first round to Chesty and the Army. Then came one for the street they lived on, another for Old Lady Fitchman, geography teacher of P.S. 149. And how could they forget General MacArthur? They had an extra because the General was Irish. Chesty was nursing his second beer. A swimming contest was being held in his stomach.

Then came the review of their staggering memoirs.

They couldn't stop laughing over Spanky Morgan, now dead, may he rest in peace, who'd call mothers on the phone around two in the morning to tell them between tears that their sons were just killed: *Bloody, horrible accident, Ma'm. The car turned over a bridge. The police are now searching for his body with dragnets. Now, Ma'm, don't worry and go right back to sleep and I'll take care of the body. I know a cheap undertaker. Gets rid of the body in no time. Well, gotta go, Ma'm. So sorry, Ma'm. And so forth, Ma'm.* And Spanky would hang up, howl and howl and sink to the floor of the telephone booth potted with laughter.

Oh, Spanky was a hot guy! One goddamn holy scream! Life of the party! Wottasensayuma! Too bad that truck hit him. He shouldn't have got so drunk. May he rest in peace, please God, give him a break, God.

Chesty wondered what ever happened to Jinx Mallon. Chuck hoped Jinx was stone dead in a ditch. Wasn't he a dirty screwball? Didn't he punch his mother inna nose? 'Magine punching your own flesh and blood's nose! That dirty pool! Oh, Christ, he was one of God's genuine punks! What happens to him should please happen to Hitler! They quickly drank to the death of Jinx Mallon. Chesty shut his eyes and permitted a snatch of beer to trinkle past his lips.

Then someone recalled the night they had Big Jenny, and how they searched high and low for a bed, and they found a bed, but Jenny was too big for the bed, and they sent her home. Oh, Jenny, did you have to be so big, so big!

A drunk came in and asked for a rye, no chaser. Chuck bent down and gave him a hotfoot. The drunk got rid of the rye, asked for another and got rid of that. In a collapsed state of soused giddiness they watched the flame of the match eat hungrily into the drunk's shoe. And then they roared and their bellies bounced behind their summer shirts when the drunk stamped his foot, killed the flame, paid for his drinks, called the guys unprintable wise guys and walked out of the bar in the full bloom of stiff dignity.

The bartender came over and said that a church was having a Sunday Night Mass down the block and wouldn't they please cut the noise. They mopped up their laughter, crossed their hearts and mumbled to God that they were good Catholics. All kidding aside, God, good Catholics.

Ed Rogers, Chuck's brother-in-law, wanted to listen to Jack Benny. The bartender said no and Ed said that Jack Benny made his girl laugh and he'd be good and goddamned if he couldn't listen to Jack Benny. One of them said they oughta break up the joint, and Chuck told the bartender just where he can shove his lousy radio, and they all bowed their heads when the bartender reminded them of the Sunday Night Mass down the block. They drank one round to the Catholic Church and God.

And then came the change in their voices, washed in mist. They walked like goons to a table, slumped in their chairs and the guy who said he'd get stewed was stewed, and he delivered a drooling lecture on topical themes:

The war and what's gonna be?

How come housepainting wasn't good enough for Hitler?

The brand of Churchill's cigars.

Who told the Japs they can play baseball?

If the Russian women pilot boats and drive tanks who in hell does the cooking?

Mahatma Ghandi's laundry bills.

Why Mussolini should use Kreml.

The Turkish situation and the food in Chinatown.

That Man in the White House.

The meat situation in relation to the French situation.

V for Victory, da, da, da, DA!

I love my wife, but oh you kid!

The Bobbsey Twins in their first whore house.

Christmas comes just once a year, mail your packages early.

I can write a helluva sonnet about my mother-in-law's Easter bonnet!

The Danish situation.

The Polish situation.

Who sells La Guardia his hats?

The hat situation.

The divorce situation in relation to Tommy Manville.

And, Jesus, wotta we gonna do about the situation in Brooklyn?

And he ended his lecture by demanding that Chesty protect the girlish virtue of the American etcetera, and he kissed him and asked to be his over-sexed grandmother, and he flopped his face into his arms, and his electricity was snuffed, and his friends wildly applauded the lecture. Chuck said he'd ship the guy home parcel post. Chesty wiped the guy's spit from his cheek.

A thin man at the bar had a ringy voice. Chesty listened to him say to the bartender: I have a great passion for sour cream and cough drops. I intend to open a restaurant. I will call it Cafe Sour Cream and Cough Drops! And, between the both of us, I travel the country collecting blood clots. Nasty hobby, these blood clots. I advise you not to go into it.

Chesty turned to his friends and they were stinko and blotto with the sheen of scotch in their faces. He thought of the next day, a new day to look at the world through grey colored binoculars, a brand new life wrapped in cellophane. He was to report at the Army Physical Induction Center, Grand Central Palace, 7 A.M. He thought of home.

Home is where you buy your misery, no cost for alteration. Pop walking his last mile. A dirty anti-Bon Ami house. Nickelodeon meals at the Automat. Joe and Skinny, the mad prince and the sad pauper. Home, home on the range, where the hands and the bodies play, where never is heard an encouraging word! Oh, go to sleep, my baby, my baby with your two brothers in one bed! And Pop saying I can't sleep in Mom's bed because it would be a sin against her soul, and Mabel railroading her bed to Washington, and Pop saying how strong I am and how strong he was and how strong I am, etcetera, etcetera. Where do we go from here, boys, where do we go from here? I'm going to the Army, and you should pardon my boyish squeal, my ecstasy, my ecstasy. A belch sprang from his stomach.

Two big fellows and a girl in a tight dress stepped up to the bar. The fellows gripped the bulge of the girl's hips tightly, closely. One slobbered her mouth with a kiss while the other pawed his way up and down her back. When one stopped his kissing, the other started. Wet, drippy kisses. Wet, drippy design for living. They called for gin and drank to the night and a bed. The girl laughed and gulped the gin.

The film of Chesty's eyes became slurry. It seemed to him that the girl wore the intimate affairs of her body as one very proudly wears a badge of honor. *Brother, this isn't purity in a big, big bottle, this master student of the University of the French Post Card.*

He tried to crush a shiver that stung his neck, and he resented the injection of a needle that jabbed swigs of desire into him when one fellow spoke of his plans when the lights go out.

The bartender asked them to please keep it clean and above board, fellows, in view of the Sunday Night Mass down the block. The sour cream and cough drop gourmet, the collector of blood clots, said that the exhibition was definitely a vulgar art form. The girl and the fellows told them where to go and what to do, variations on a theme.

They finished their drinks and resumed the act of the kiss and the clutch, and vice-versa. Chesty said what the hell and walked to the bar and compared his physical culture to one of the fellows. *Big guy, a longshoreman, a subway guard, a third-rate heavyweight. Couldn't be a clerk. Clerks are tiny people who drink double-rich malteds and fig newtons.* He ordered a beer.

The girl said that Nature was calling her to the John, and she said that they should come back later, and if Big Jack was around the hotel, well, they should bring him along, Sweet Big Jack. She strutted to the ladies room, her hips moving so slow and easy. *I got rhythm, I got rhythm, I got rhythm, who could ask for anything more.*

The big fellows left with words on why her hips should be entered in contests, and the bartender said: thank God. He drew a beer and piously spoke of the Holy Virgin.

Chesty paid for the beer, placed it to his lips with a lament and a prayer, and the bitterness of it sprayed wrinkles over his face. The bar became alive with new voices. A little man with a cigar and a little woman asked for scotch. A boy asked if Barney Reynolds was here and the bartender shook his head and the boy walked out and said that he was pretty sick and tired of looking for his drunken Uncle Barney, pretty sick and tired.

The little woman combed her hair over her scotch, and the little man with the cigar registered a complaint. The woman said that scotch with dandruff was good for the liver, and the man grunted: shut up! And the woman wept.

The man said: Will you shut up?

The woman said: Go to hell very quickly! Go now!

The man said: Is that the way you talk to the man who loves you, Dolly?

The woman's body heaved and the cigar in the man's mouth heaved and they embraced each other over their scotch.

The door of the ladies room opened and the girl with the tight dress took her place at the bar. Chesty's eyes darted over her body like one taking inventory of rare stock, the world's oldest vintage. He wondered what the material of her dress felt like. And then came the itch to splash his hands over her body, to give her something to remember him by. *Oh, Beatrice Fairfax, please tell me the bare facts.* He felt the discharge of a new voice, voice control was not his forte at the moment.

He said: Hot night.

She said: That's your story.

She had wise eyes. Her lips were pursed. A vein clung to her neck. She smiled wisely. *Tell me why you smile, Mona Lisa?*

He said: My name's Chesty, Chesty Anderson.

She said: Hello, Chesty Anderson.

He said: Don't look now, but you're getting to be a habit with me.

She let her body touch his. His legs buckled.

She said: How you talk, Mr. Anderson.

How Mr. Anderson wanted to talk!

He wanted to say something exquisitely clever, something clever enough to sweep her off her spiked heels. And then he would want her to say: how clever you are, Chesty, how clever.

But she maneuvered her body closer to his and he felt her bulge and his tongue became lumpy and starched and his hands shimmied and zing went the string of his voice. She stepped away. The maneuver was completed. She motioned for him to follow her. He did.

Oh, tis love and love alone the world is seeking.

There was a table in the far back of the room. It was dark, and she sat down and he sat down next to her. He saw the black streak that ran down her blonde hair, and he wanted to pile his face into her hair and recite toilet wall poetry. She put out her hand and he kissed it. *Pale hands I love beside the Shalimar.* She pulled her chair closer. He kissed the vein in her neck.

She said: Read any good books lately?

And then he kissed her the way those fellows kissed her. And then he kissed her the way that matinee-idol kissed that ingenue. And then he kissed her the way that Spanish girl kissed him last New Year's Eve. And then he thought of the fellows' toast to a night and a bed and their plans when the lights go out, and he felt the rash of a tremble in his body, and she felt the tremble, and she calmly patted his head.

She said: You need a woman.

He said: I'd like to sign you up for ninety-nine years.

She said: You sound like Busch's Credit Jewelers.

He kissed her mouth and spoke into it.

He said: If a trip around the world cost a dime I wouldn't get as far as Hoboken. Translation: I'm broke.

She said: No lend-lease, today. Not today.

He said: Give me a crack at you, Miss. I'll come around after the war and pay the bill.

She said: Say, who the hell writes your scripts?

He said:. Trust me, Miss. I'm an honest John.

She pushed him away. Her face was as hard as a mask. She saw her lipstick smeared over his lips. She thought of a circus clown she once laughed at. *Funny little clown with the red lips and the white face and the sad eyes.*

She said: Charity begins at home!

He said: Give me my last fling before joining the Army.

She said: In my line it's pay-as-you-enter! No tickee, no washee! Velly solly!

She got up and he got up with her. He again pleaded for a last fling: Hell, what have you got to lose? Am I not going to war to fight for your right to drink gin and search for Sweet Big Jacks in dirty bars?

She felt a roll of spit in her mouth and, God, she knew what she wanted to do with it, but she didn't do it. She swallowed it and cursed him, and he quivered and jammed his hands down her back and felt the flesh above her stockings, and she felt his starchy fingers tearing her flesh, and she cracked his face, and his eyes winked from the sting.

She said: I'll break your head, you helluva dumb bastard!

He tried to soothe the swell of his face. He wanted to ask her to sit down, Miss, and talk things over. *What is this thing called love, this funny thing called love?* But the bartender's voice called her name and said that two fellows were asking for her. She pulled up her stockings. The red welts of his fingerprints excited him.

He said: Stay awhile. Can't you stay awhile? Do you have to go out there and leave me in here dying for you?

She said: Listen, you, you boob! My business is out there! Don't ruin my business!

She walked out into the light of the bar and left him sitting in the darkness, and he heard the loud tones of the fellows greet her and ask for gin. *East is East and West is West and never the twain shall meet.* He heard her laugh. His face twitched. Once a friend told him about an abortion. He was never able to forget the pressure of that conversation. The friend said that his sister went to a man who scraped her cells and tissues and the flesh that was forming into a child. Then the friend cried and said that his sister died. Chesty felt scraped. Yes, dead. Young man, young victim of an abortion. *Oh, shove over, sister!*

He walked slowly out of the darkness and saw her flitting from one fellow to the other. She was drinking and they were watching her drain her gin, and when he passed he yearned for the guts to break the glass over her head, to split her ear with the scream that he broke the glass, he broke the glass. He, he did it, and what about it? But the spirit that produces guts was too barren for revival. *Thanks for the memory, it was a lovely day.*

He went to his friends and two of them were mutilating a popular song. Chuck was having a very engrossing conversation with Chuck, and he regretted very confidentially to Chuck that he had but only one Chuck to give his Chuck. Chesty asked if they were going. They continued their mutilation. Chesty said he was calling the night a day. He walked out of the bar. *Show me the way to go home. I'm tired and wanna go to bed.*

He breathed in and out and the hot air made him think of how nice it would be to be by the sea, by the sea, by the beautiful sea. He looked through the window of the bar and saw the girl and the two fellows walking out. He quickly crossed the street and they crossed the street, and he quickly walked up the street and they slowly walked up the street, and he crossed to the other side and saw the trio enter a rooming house. *You're gonna miss me, honey.* Like hell you will, honey! He lit a cigaret and thanked her violently for such tender memories.

A girl passed him. *Barefoot girl with cheeks of rouge.* He followed her and her bare legs made him thirst for a girl of his own and only his own and all his own and when the hell was he going to have a girl of his own, a girl he can kiss and make love to and buy things for and talk to and walk with and marry and have a kid and another kid. *I will take you home, Kathleen.*

The girl with the bare legs entered a drugstore. He thought he'd better go home and get some sleep. He was to join the Army the next morning, 7 A.M. He recalled the jukebox recording of three Negroes and a guitar:

There'll be a change in the weather
And a change in the scene,
From now on there'll be a change in me.
My walk will be different,
My talk and my name,
Nothing about me's gonna be the same.

I'm gonna change my way of living
And if that ain't enough
I'm gonna change the way I strut my stuff.
'Cause nobody wants you when you're old and grey,
There'll be some changes made today,

There'll be some changes made.

Tomorrow at 7 A.M. *Oh, there will be a helluva lot of changes in the life of Citizen Chesty Anderson!*

The concentrated hot air made the beer in his stomach spin. He stepped into a bus. The bus-driver's face was blurry. Chesty wanted to vomit.

CHAPTER 14

THE OLD man walked down the dirty, dark stairway. In the street he reread the sign that drew him to the decayed tenement building, one flight up:

MADAME ZAVETTE

The Madame reads your life, past, present and future. She asks no questions, but tells exactly what you wish to know. She tells the truth, good or bad, on all affairs of life, love, health, the heart, marriage, courtship, divorce, wealth and business transactions of all kinds. She never fails to reunite the separated. She is the cause of speedy and happy marriages. Her advice will overcome bad luck of all kinds and enemies of all kinds. She will help you win and hold the one you love till the day you die. Consult the Madame! Hours: 9 to 9. Readings: $2.

The drive of a decision to go back and demand his money back incited the acid in his mind, but he spit at the sign and called the Madame a stinking fake, oh, such a stinking fake. *Oh, tell me pretty Madame, are there anymore at home like you?* He entered a corner bar.

He asked for a beer and studied his face through a mirror and

saw a delicate network of lines crisscross his face, and he touched
the patches of light blue pigment taped under his eyes, and the
rapid terror of his old age peering at him so placidly caused one
jitter to multiply into many. He turned to his beer for consolation.

The bar was crowded with men and smoke, and a Chinaman
was playing a piano. *In a little Spanish town 'twas on a night like
this.*

The old man looked around and saw a midget with a red, drip-
ping nose ask a waitress if, please, was it possible to get a glass of
hot milk?

The waitress, her hair in bobby pins, and lacquered curls pasted
tightly to her scalp, said: Hot milk? Do you mean the stuff kids
drink?

The midget said: If I can get a glass of hot milk and, please, a
little butter in the milk, I'd be the happiest man in the world.

The waitress said: But who drinks hot milk at a bar?

The midget said: You can see for yourself that I got a cold, Miss.

The waitress said: A cafeteria's onna corner! Go there! Hurry
up! Hot milk with butter! For Christ's sake!

The midget blew his red nose and left his table. The waitress
called out: Get inna hot bed! Drink hot tea with lemon! Hot tea
with lemon! Lottsa lemon! Lottsa tea! Don't forget it! Hot milk
with butter! Howdaya like that?

The midget thanked her very, very much for her knowledge,
and the old man replaced the midget at the table, and the waitress
sang out his request for beer and waddled her bulky beef to a table
where three strong men were noisy and smelly with the snapping
odor of whiskey. One of them rubbed her behind.

She said: Wottahell's the big idea!

The man said: It's for luck.

She said: Rub your wife's ass for luck and see how she likes it!

They spewed large doses of howls in her face, and she called
their order and told one of them just what he could do when he said

that Benny sent him.

She came back with a tray, three whiskeys and a beer. She placed the whiskey on the strong men's table and handed the old man his beer. He paid her and her fleshy fingers nimbly scooped up his coin. The raw stink of her perfume excited him. Her low-slung breasts made him think of stale bread.

The face of one of the strong men puzzled the old man. He walked over with his beer. He asked if his name was Sam Duncan.

The man said: Hell, no! Never heard of the guy, Pop!

The old man said: You look like Sam. Same long nose.

The man said: Do me a favor and leave my nose outa this!

Another said: Join us, Pop.

The old man said: Glad to.

The other said: They're always picking on my nose!

They got to talking about the War and Defense, and they worked for a tool plant up the block, good pay and time and a half on Sunday, but that foreman, oh, that miserable phony of a fore- man was a dirty Greek punk. *When day is done and shadows fall we think of you,* you dirty Greek punk! They promised faithfully to give him a workout the hour the Armistice was signed. They had a lot of words for the Greek.

One of them said: No time for workout now! This is war! Every man is vital! Including Greeks!

Another said: I swear by my mother to pull the leg out of his ass on Armistice Day!

They cursed the Greek in seven delicious flavors and felt secure and happy over his future without a leg, and the old man thought it would be friendly to laugh along, but Jesus, he felt too old to laugh. Laughter was a strong man's monopoly. He cackled.

After a few beers a warm, thick emotion caked-up in the old man. He listened to the men speak of love, life and Greek foremen, and why a man's not a man without a woman, and he watched the waitress move from table to table. *I wanna big fat mamma.*

One man said: Pop, how's your woman?

The old man said: I'm a man without a woman. I was married. Now she's dead. I hate my life without my wife.

The man said: I hate my life without my wife! That's poetry! Damn fine, beautiful, damn fine, beautiful poetry!

Another said: Wottahellayou know about poetry?

The other said: Yeah, since when?

The man said: I ought to know poetry! My daughter writes poetry! You should see my daughter's poetry!

They drank to the daughter who was a poet. They included the old man's poetic ability. *The Poet Laureate of Slattery's Bar and Grill.* The old man bowed and wondered what the hell it was all about.

The waitress was called over to give her frank, nothing but her frank opinion on life.

She said: Life stinks merrily!

The old man said: Have you a man, Miss?

She said: I wouldn't give a plugged nickel for the best of them!

One of the men said: Where do you get off, you fat bum! I'm a man! I wouldn't leak on your grave!

She said: Show respect to an American lady, you filthy foreigner, you!

He said: Foreigner, my eye! My family fought in the Revolution!

She said: So you're a dirty sonuva revolution!

He said: Get killed, you fat crummy bum!

Another said: Pick up your ass, it's falling!

The other said: If I weren't a gentleman I'd slug the hell outa you!

The waitress fled to the back, her breasts swinging and her eyes watering.

One man said: Pop, 95% of the women are no damn good! The only 5% who are any damn good are our mothers and sisters!

The old man said: I can cry when I see a woman cry.

The man said: No flea bag's calling me a filthy foreigner!

Another said: Don't waste tears on fat ladies, Pop!

The other said: The customer's always right, Pop!

The waitress came back and her face was freshly powdered and her eye rims were red. She asked what they'd have to drink. They ignored her. She asked again and they delivered a double-talk routine on the waterfall condition of Niagara Falls in view of the scarcity of strawberries in the Arctic Zone, and don't forget the fyoonasetic on the flattersteen when you enter the Port of Bali-Bali. The old man hated to see a woman with red eyes. He said he'd have a beer. She thanked him very impressively, and very loudly.

Suddenly the men and their chairs shifted into a tight knot, and they outlawed the old man by stage-whispering to themselves in tones charged with flame.

The old man ached to squirm out of the existing cordon sanitaire, but the fear and the sting of being scorned at for running away forced him to assemble a portion of guts for the hard purpose of crossing his legs and waiting for his beer. The waitress set it before him. He paid her and wondered how she'd look undressed. *I wanna big fat mamma, big and round.*

One of the men turned to him. His lips jumped over his teeth as he spoke. The old man thought of an angry dog he once kicked.

The man said: Who in hell invited you?

The old man said: I thought you were Sam Duncan.

The man said: I wouldn't be found dead with Sam Duncan!

Another said: And who the frig is Sam Duncan?

The old man said: A steelworker from East St. Louis. I worked with him.

One man said: Where do you get off working inna steelmill, you old bum?

The other said: And where do you get off saying my pal's gotta long nose?

The old man said: If I had my strength I'd break all your backs.

One said: Oh, jump inna river! Drown yourself!

Another said: You're stinking up the joint!

The other said: Screw, bum!

The piano stopped.

A coat of whitewash swabbed the old man's face. He saw the bulbous power in their arms. He saw the unified cruelty in their drunken faces. He wondered where Chesty was.

One of the men spit in his beer, and the old man snapped from his chair frozen to the neurosis of being a victim to a prescribed treatment, something old, nothing new. *Memories, memories of the long ago.*

He started to leave when the stun of a trip dropped him to his knees. He arose punched with shock, and he was tripped again, and a madness spun webs in his eyes, and the animal orgasm to fight back and kill was prominent, but the equipment to fight back was nil, and the energy of a kick sent him stumbling to the floor, and the men heaved with the peculiar roar of excitement that clamps itself on people who are captivated by the obscene tapestry of violence. *God rest ye merry gentlemen.*

One said: Boys, we're practicing up for that Greek foreman!

Another said: See where I kicked him? Right inna spine!

The other said: When Armistice Day comes we'll be in great shape!

The old man sat on the floor retching pain over the physical orgy. He saw the men suffering with the want of him to rise. He slowly looked around the room, the pain squealing through his dizzy head. He saw a confusing pattern of eyes watching and estimating his next move as if he were a dumb, numb, insensitive plaything for wild children to torture. He crawled to his knees and was savagely booted and his face smeared into the sawdust of the floor. The waitress shrilled. It wrenched the taut lid of the men's sport: Leave the poor old man alone!

She helped him to his feet and wiped his face with her apron. *I wanna big fat mamma to tell my troubles to.* He impulsively wanted to tell her that they couldn't have done this to him years ago. *Oh, no! God, no! No, no!* But the growth of his humiliation was too deep, and his voice refused to comply with his impulse.

He shuffled out of the bar, a hollow man. He heard one of the men say to the waitress: Well, wottaya waiting for, you fat bum? Some whiskey! The customer's always right!

The horrible shriek of their laughter boiled pots of sweat on his back. *Where the hell was Chesty?*

The summer night plundered the light of the moon, and he stumbled in the darkness, and a desolation seemed to have ruptured all his natural resources and rendered him a shredded relic. *Such was the wreck of the Hesperus in the midnite and the heat.*

He watched the swing of his gaunt arms as he walked, and he saw his poker face and dried-up, meatless figure through the windows of an auction shop. He stopped to gaze at himself, and a bitterness and a helplessness made him want to smash and stamp into tiny, pebbly particles the window that taunted him with his scarecrow reflection, the candid reflection of a grim caricature. *Leave the poor old man alone!* He cried a little.

He crossed the street and a panhandler bummed him for a dime. A lady in a stained dress asked him if he was in the mood for the time of his life.

He said: No, thank you, lady

She said: I'm good for what ails you, mister.

He walked away and thought of what ailed him. He thought of his wife and the nights he'd go to her bed and whisper for her to move over. *Move over, Sylvia, move over.* Then he'd press his hands over her weary, punctured body in the dark and she'd cling to him and he'd feel her body grow tingly and full, and he'd feel the sizzle of warm spots shooting in her skin, and he'd be silent and she'd be silent, and he'd be tired and she'd be tired, and he'd say goodnight,

goodnight, Sylvia, and he'd climb into his bed and into the green pasture of sleep. Then he remembered the fat waitress and her flat breasts. *Nobody loves a fat woman, but oh how a fat woman can love.*

I'll go back and I'll drink beer and I'll tell her I was once an iron man, chest like a barrel and packed full of muscle. She'll believe me and say: oh, ain't it a helluva dirty shame you lost your strength, your beautiful strength. Yes, ain't it a helluva dirty shame. And I'll tell her about Chesty and his muscles, my son with the muscles I owned. And I'll ask her who's taking her home, and she'll say: why, you're taking me home, Harry. And, goddamn, I will take her home, and I'll undress her because she'll be so tired from a hard day's work, and she'll thank me for my kindness. I'll go back someday. I will.

He opened the door of his house. He went to his room, undressed and toyed with the carnal idea of how the fat waitress would like the empty bed that belonged to his wife. *You'd be so nice to come home to.* He wet his lips.

He washed his hands and quietly opened the door of his sons' bedroom. He looked down on Chesty, Joe and Skinny. The room was stuffy and the three were sleeping in the nude. He saw the relaxed, flexible bands of power in Chesty's arms, legs, chest. This naked body, he thought, was his donation to his son, and he thought of the three men in the bar and a grip choked his neck. *Here, here was Chesty.*

He left the room, stepped into his bed, looked at the shadowy walls and realized that in a few hours his son would be leaving for the Army. He wondered what life and home would be like without his son, and a melange of loneliness and gladness and sadness, and a swift tug of pride ripped the cloth of his body, and he felt chilly in the hot room. He pulled the blanket up to his eyes and began a silent conversation with his wife about the way things are and the way they were going and how he missed her and how was she getting along and did she miss him. *Oh, how I miss you tonight, more than you'll ever know.*

A cavalcade of sketchy flights of thought congregated its variety of postures in the room, and from them all came the emergence of the fat waitress toting her perfumed body, and he desperately looked at the empty bed in the room, and he was able to feel the juicy presence of her body draped in the bed that wasn't empty anymore. *Move over, Miss, move over.* And then came the swift reaction of his wife and children that came from his wife. He ended his conversation with the waitress at once, apologized to his wife, plunged his face under the blanket, his lips wet and shaky. He felt very guilty.

CHAPTER 15

THE AVERAGE temperature in the city yesterday was ninety-seven degrees, the highest ever established on July 18, exceeding by one degree the average of ninety-six reached in 1925. However, the temperature was two degrees short of the record established in 1919. The Weather Bureau predicts a rise in temperature for today, said *The New York Times.*

Seven in the morning.

The man at the Local Draft Board said: This is a government token. It will allow you free train fare to the induction center, Grand Central Palace. Your group captain is Dominick Roggliano, Dominick Roggliano. Stay with your group captain, Dominick Roggliano.

The train, bulging tin cans for sardines, human brand.
Push, push, push!

Headlines in your face: RUSSIANS TAKE THIRTY MORE TOWNS. VIOLENCE IN BUDAPEST. GIANTS TRIM DODGERS. RUMORED PEACE TALKS. MAN MURDERS WIFE AND LOVER.

Push, push, push!

Vanities of the underground: Solidified sweat oozing from the armpit, the feet and melting makeup. The hysterical pierce of train wheels stabbing unprepared ears.

Push, push, push!

Mouth smells in production: oatmeal, eggs, coffee, last night's garlic and fish, last night's beer, this morning's pickled sardines.

Push, push, push!

Weary blues: tired bodies, tired eyes, tired hands clutching straps and bars, tired legs, sweltering lipstick on tired mouths, tired brains.

Push, push, push!

The hot whispers of conversation: I remember when her hair was black.   Got an aspirin? My boss, he should hang.   The war'll be over in six months! . . .   That's definite!   Oh, baby, you're for me!   Say, how's that tall brother of yours?   I'll die if I'm late! Miriam still got labor pains?   Wottsanamayabook?   I hate cops! Sid's at Camp Shelby.   Over my dead body he'll get his ring back! Oh, how I hate to get up inna morning. . . . Oh, how I love to lie in bed.   She's too good for him!   He's from hunger!   Marie's marrying a Jew!   How's business, Mr. Fenster?   Her little boy was run over and she went to the movies the same night with that same man!   I'm taking an aviation course!   Irv'n I go steady.   The papers reported him missing in Italy.   Kill alla Germans, that's my solution!   Rhoda's gotta baby, Janet's gotta baby, and I gotta boyfriend who talks about Betty Grable when I talk about marriage

and babies.   She struggled for him and what did she get!   Look what's by the door? . . . Wotta piece of meat! I can't stand the living sight of him!   Wouldn't you love a home in the country?
     Push, push, push!

Americans in limbo: man with a boil, terrified schoolgirl, boy with beard, lady with asthma, old man with glasses, old lady with blackheads and garden variety of pimples, young girl with glasses eyeing old man with glasses, exotic oriental from the Bronx.
     Push, push, push!

It pays to advertise: GOOD TO THE LAST DROP.   POLLY PINK-HAM'S PURPLE PILLS FOR PALE FACES.   BE THIN! . . . WEAR A THREE-WAY STRETCH.   DON'T BE THE ACME OF ACNE.   MUM'S THE WORD.   TRY OUR FRIENDLY LAXATIVE.   CONCERTS IN CENTRAL PARK.   EAT WHEATIES.   BUY A BOND.   SMOKE CAMELS.   MEET MISS SUBWAY.   EVEN YOUR BEST FRIENDS WON'T TELL YOU.   NOW YOU CAN BE TALLER THAN SHE. . . . WEAR ELEVATED SHOES.   HOW'S YOUR LIVER BILE?
     Push, push, push!

Forty-second Street!

Stay with your group captain, Dominick Roggliano, Dominick Roggliano!

The streets and the building stand still and bored and the girls and the boys and the men and the women and the buses on the ground and the trains under the ground race uptown and down-town and around the corner.

Wholesale and retail communiques: PLEASE HELP THE BLIND. BREAKFAST, 15C AND UP.   REDUCTION ON SHIRTS.   WATCHES

REPAIRED.   WE LOAN MONEY.   REDUCTION ON DRESSES.   LET US FURNISH YOUR HOME.   MORNING NEWS, MIRROR, WOTTAYA READ?   THE DAWN COMES EARLY EVERY MORNING, FIFTH SENSATIONAL WEEK.   PLEASE HELP THE BLIND,

And the streets and the buildings stand still and bored . . .

There's Grand Central Palace! *Don't shoot until you see the whites of their eyes!*

A sergeant said: Okay, you guys, line up! This is a Government building and while you're here you gotta obey Army regulations! Now get rid of your newspapers and cut out the smoking! Strip and check your clothes and tie the check around your neck! When you hear your name called step up and get your papers and hold onto them tight! Keep your eyes open and your mouth shut and act alive! Let's go!

Think they'll take me with sinus, Mac?   Last summer I broke my wrist.   Know what I think? . . . I think I'ma neurotic.   My cough ain't funny.   Only last summer I was in 3A.   Two years ago I had the clap.   I support my mother and sister.   My wife's pregnant.   Maybe I ain't got bum eyes.   A doctor said I got an obstruction in my nose.   I'll trade my lousy teeth for anything you got.   Day in, day out my throat's always sore.   I have trouble breathing.   You got high blood pressure? . . . I ain't got blood! Flat feet don't mean a thing.   Yeah, I know they don't take them in, but who's a homosexual?   Hey, Bud, wennaya think the war'll end?

The sergeant said. All right, line up you guys who are stripped! Walk through that door, obey orders and don't lose your papers and everything will be all right! Shake it up and get going!

Chesty's head bounced with confusion. *Line up, obey regulations, get rid of your newspapers, check your clothes, no smoking, step up, get your papers, keep your eyes open, keep your mouth shut, shake it up, get going.* He walked through the door, confused and naked. *This is the Army, Mister Jones.*

This scale for your height and weight! Step up! Next!

Open your mouth. Keep it open. Open it wider. All right. Next!

Cover your right eye with your right hand and read the third line on the chart. Now cover your left eye. That's all. Next!

Can you hear this? thirty-one, forty-eight, sixty-three, ninety-two, seventy-six. Ear's okay. Next!

Bend down and spread your cheeks. Next!

Let's see your feet. Come on, relax. Good. Next!

If anyone here is physically handicapped please report to Room 327. I repeat: if anyone here is physically handicapped please report to Room 327.

Cough. Does it hurt? Cough. Cough. That's the idea. Cough again. Do you lift heavy things at work? Does it pain you when you lift heavy things? You're okay. Next!

You fellows wait in line. Don't come in for your x-ray until you see someone walk out who has been x-rayed. Let's have no trouble. This is very important. When you see someone leave, one of you come in, hand your papers to the clerk in uniform and await orders. Let's have no trouble!

Attention everybody: Each one of you will be given a bottle to urinate in. This will determine if you have gonorrhea or not. After you fill the bottle, bring it back to me. Now do as I say and let it run smooth. Okay!

Do you hear sounds at night?   Do you think people talk about you?   When people laugh in the street do you think they are laughing at you?   What do you do for a living?   Do you like your work?   Do you resent taking orders?   Do crowds annoy you? Do you have nervous disorders?   Is it easy to disturb you?   Do you get along with your friends?   What do you think of this war? What papers do you read?   Did you ever wet your bed?   When did you last have a girl?   Did you feel weak after it happened?   Do you think girls like you?   Do you think some hate you?   Did you ever have relations with a man?   I mean, did you ever go to bed with a man?   Next!

The sergeant said: All right, you guys, the examination's over! Hand your check in and get your clothes and dress and go to the big room on the left and wait for your name to be called! Now listen carefully: When your name's called, step up and get your papers and walk down the hall to the desks on the right! When you get there get in single line and hand your papers to the men behind the desks! These men will tell you what to do and what's what! Now if any one of you guys don't understand, please speak up now! Speak up now! Let's go!

It's all over. Sue me, but I couldn't spring a leak.   Of course it's easy to disturb me.   Tell me I stink and see how I'm disturbed. When they take me in with my bum eyes they don't care who joins the Army.   He asks one guy what papers he reads. The guy says *The Racing Form*.   Bend down and spread your cheeks. How about that?   I told him some girls like Dorothy like me and some girls like Clara hate me. He said that's natural. Wottahell's so natural about it?   Don't get in the artillery. It's murder in the artillery.   I hear sounds at night, all right. My damn wife snores.   The way the doc looked up my ass you'd think I was hiding a German submarine.   Like I told my Mamma: Momma, my new trade is killing Nazis, the pay is good, but the hours stink.   I can drive. I'll apply for ambulance corps.   I like my work, I told him. But my boss don't like my work.   I gotta pal inna Medical Corps. Georgie, he said, it's murder inna Medical Corps.   He asked me if I liked being alone. Sure, Doc, I said, alone with a blonde.   When do you get paid in the Army?   Hey, answer me! Do all Japs grin and wear thick glasses?   I can't make up my mind if khaki suits my personality.   Did I ever go to bed with a man! What goes on here? We're in the Army now. We'll never get rich. Period.   Hey, Bud, wennaya think the war'll end?

They finished dressing, went to the big room, heard their names called, received their papers and walked down the hall in single file. They stopped in front of the desks.

One by one, they handed their papers to the men behind the desks. The men studied each paper, reached for a stamp, stamped a white slip and told them to go to the room behind them and await orders. One fellow was given a yellow slip. He was told to use the stairway on the right.

Chesty handed the man his papers. The man looked it over, looked at Chesty and stamped a yellow slip. He was told to use the stairway on the right.

A bewilderment stitched dots and lines in Chesty's face. He walked away and read the yellow slip. YOU HAVE BEEN REJECTED BY THE UNITED STATES ARMED FORCES.

He walked back to the desk, and it seemed like a long journey. He wanted to know about the words written on the yellow slip, how come and what's up.

The man looked at his papers and said: You have a weak heart, son. Take it easy.

4F!

Sometimes I feel like a motherless child, a long way from home.

CHAPTER 16

THE SUN was hot and he saw two soldiers coming down the street, and he felt the collapse of his legs and the severe nausea of shrinking, and the light of the day turned into a dark room, and he stood stiff and scared in the dark room, and the soldiers passed and the darkness passed, and he watched their big backs facing the sun. *There, but for the grace of Grand Central Palace, go I.* He searched his pockets for a cigaret. He knew he had none. But he searched.

He walked down the street and down another street and up a street and down a street and the streets went on and on, ending in a gutter and starting on a sidewalk, a gloomy merry-go-round of pavement, cement without end.

Summertime, and the living is easy.

The steamroom of the summer day made a soggy rag of his shirt and soggy jelly of his insides, and a vital pain split his head, and he was oblivious of frustrating a biological lollipop with delicately trimmed eyebrows, who smiled as if it were an exclusive design created solely for his face. A piping swish bathed his voice: My apartment is nearby, dear boy. Do come up. And the drinks I mix! They are truly darling. And my Flamenco recordings! Oh, I know you'll just think them superb! I tell you they are luscious, simply luscious. Come up, dear boy. Do!

The streets rose and fell, and the sun lost its sting. A consciousness prodded his head. He saw the oasis of Union Square flanked by the perspiring quicksands of Klein's, Ohrbach's and the Manufacturer's Trust Company. He flopped on a bench. A man was talking about the war and the position of Finland, and how something or other was stinky in Helsinki. Chesty held his head in his hands to control the sway of his pain, and the pitch of the man's voice was like a grinding saw cutting and cutting its way through the belly of a tree. *Where do we go from here, boys, where do we go from here?* He fell asleep.

A warm wind blew up, and he got up.

A man said to his child: A sunshower will cool things off, Bernie. A sunshower is the sun's worst enemy. That's nature for you.

Men in shirtsleeves were listening to a man expounding the dialectics of the health and poverty of nations, and what to do about it. A girl was scolding two sailors. A kid was proudly displaying a leg scab to a bored cop. A dog slept by the statue of Abe Lincoln.

Chesty plodded to the subway. *Stay with your group captain, Dominick Roggliano, Dominick Roggliano.* He wondered if Dominick Roggliano had a weak heart, too.

CHAPTER 17

Come back to Erin, my darling, my darling. Be it ever so humble there is no place like Erin, home, home, the warehouse of his unlaughing boyhood.

He reached his house, went to his room, sat on his bed for awhile, went to the kitchen, looked for food, found an apple and a roll, brought it to his room, sat on his bed, heard the door open, saw Joe come in, bit into the apple and then the roll and suddenly felt the beat of his heart, a new instrument to remember, the beat of his heart, the click, the beat, the tick. No, the clang. Yes, the clang, the clang of his heart. That's it. That's it, all right. The clang of his heart. A new instrument to remember. You are not aware of it until you are told of it. He was told of it. *Gone are the dear days, days beyond recall.* Joe came into the room.

He said: My big brother, the soldier.

Chesty said: I was rejected.

He said: Wottaya handing me?

Chesty said: I have a weak heart.

He said: But you're a strong guy!

Chesty said: Yeah.

He said: You 4F? You?

Chesty said: Me.

He said: No!

Chesty said: Yes.

He said: Goddamn!

Chesty said: Goddamn.

He said: What's Pop gonna say?

What's Pop gonna say? What's Pop gonna say?

Joe said he had to leave. He said he had to run somewhere. Chesty heard him run down the stairs. Running somewhere. Running down stairs. Running anywhere. Running, running. Run, little children. Run, run the hundred yard dash. Once he ran the hundred yard dash. A luxury these days. A lost art these days. A lost art for weak hearts. *What's Pop gonna say?*

Yeah, what's Pop gonna say? I'm his youth, he says, his strength. He'll show me how to lift pianos. He'll show me how to lift nothing, that's what he'll show me! And who the hell cares what Pop has to say? What can I say, that is the question? To lift a piano or not to lift a piano, that is the question. Oh, God, me, the conquering hero with a bum heart. Sir Galahad with a bum heart. Not good for the Army. Good for nothing. Not even good for the Johnson Motor Company. Strictly a misfit, my boy. Out of this world, Jack. Get in line for a soft job. Test rocking chairs. Make notes on its swing. Come home clean from work. White collar in the morning, white collar at night. And don't forget the polka dot tie. White collars and polka dot ties.

Look forward to white collars and polka dot ties. That is fate and your future. And what's Pop gonna say to that? That is the goddamn question!

You are not aware of it until you are told of it.

Well, what this country needed was a good five cent heart. Oh, be brave about the whole thing. You're not going to throw in the sponge, are you? Hell, no, not you! Valiant is the word for Chesty! Sure, the beans are tough and the meat is fat, and oh, my Lord, you can't eat that. But there is always milk and crackers, crackers and milk. And what's wrong with tea and lemon? On the level, what's wrong with tea and lemon? Of course you'll have to go to sleep early. You won't be able to smoke. You'll have to sit under trees and say to hell with the sun. For Christmas a good friend will buy you a cane and fur-lined slippers. Why, you'll get a great big kick out of settling down nice and easy under a tree and never getting excited about anything at all. And then there is the subject of girls. Whatever you do, whatever you do, Chesty, leave the girls alone. Kiss the girls good-bye. That's a must on your program. So be brave about the whole thing. Say, after all, you only have fifty years ahead of you. What's fifty years in a shot-to-hell life? Say that over and over again and you'll see what I mean. So what can Pop say? Think it over. What the hell can he say? Did you ask for a bum heart? Did you pick it out of a Sears-Roebuck catalogue? Did you petition Congress for a bum heart? Well, did you? Answer that sixty-four dollar question! And Chesty, let's get down to business and look this thing straight in the face: who, the goddamn wants to lift pianos anyway?

You are not aware of it until you are told of it.

He was attracted by the beat of the clock in the kitchen, and he walked into the kitchen and saw the second hand of the clock take a walk around the numbers and settle down at twelve, and he placed the clock to his ear, placed his hand to his heart and compared the beat of the clock to the beat of his heart, and he went back to his room with the clock to his ear and hand to his heart.

He sat on the bed and sat there and sat there moving his lips and his fingers to keep time of the two rhythms, and he looked around, and his eyes searched the room, and the stillness of the room and the whiteness of the walls violated his growing anguish, and the anguish scrambled and leaped, and its momentum distorted the room, and he threw his apple at the wall, and the juice splattered and changed the color of the wall, and he threw his roll out of the window, and he punched and punched the pillow, shook the bed, slammed the door, ripped his shirt, shut the window, spit at the wall, spit at the picture of his childhood and the room swelled with the fury of his screams, and he dug his fingers into his cheeks, and he dug his teeth into his tongue to obstruct his screams, and he fell to the edge of the bed, and he panted convulsively, and a limpness congested him, and he watched the rapid throb of his chest, and he reached for the clock and placed it to his ear, and he placed his hand to his heart, and his lips and fingers moved to keep time of the two rhythms. *Two hearts beat in three-quarter time.*

Now, now, Chesty, don't get excited. Is that the way for a grown boy to act? Take it easy. Yes, yes, take it easy, slow and easy. You know, Chesty, you can't afford to get excited. It doesn't pay in the long run. Doesn't pay dividends. No, Chesty, no. Tell you what, Chesty? How about an afternoon nap? Nothing like a good old nap, nothing. Every hour on the hour, a nap. Call it a beauty sleep. That's a much prettier name. And when you get up and feel like reaching for a cigaret, why, simply reach for a pill. Will the pill replace the cigaret? Sure, no doubt about it! And while we're on the subject we must again consider the subject of girls, girls, the girls, the pretty girls who are like melodies. Just forget their soft bodies moving behind their summer dresses. Hell, simply regard them as not existing. The world's full of men from now on. That's the way to look at the thing. It's really as simple as that. Can you honestly say there is anything more simple? Well, can you? So, Chesty, old man, do all these things. Make it your life's work. You must, Chesty, you must. Goddamn, Chesty, do

you hear, you must! You do it and like it! No backtalk! Keep quiet.
Silence is essential during the run of your life! Shut up! Do it and like
it and close your mouth and close your hungry eyes! You don't want
to die, do you? Well, answer me! Do you?

You are not aware of it until you are told of it.

Yeah. *There'll be a change in the weather,*
And a change in the scene,
And from now on there'll be a change in me.
My walk will be different,
My talk and my name,
Nothing about me's gonna be the same.

I'm gonna change my way of living, all right.

You are not aware of it until you are told of it.

CHAPTER 18

Now is the time *for all good foes to come to the aid of their fathers.*

It was lunch hour and he saw the sharp bones of the old man
snap mechanically on a sandwich. He ran into the lunch wagon, his
eyes transporting fever.

He said: Pop!

The old man said: Joe? Wottaya doing here?

Joe said: Pop, I gotta talk to you!

The old man said: Wottsamatta, Joe?

Joe said: Listen, Pop! Are you listening?

The old man said: Oh, Joe! Come on! Say it!

Joe said: Pop, the Army don't want Chesty!

A mute, agonizing look stuck out of the old man's face, and Joe
told him what Chesty had told him, and the old man wanted Joe
to say it again, again, but his throat became bulky and the words
struggled and died in his throat, and he felt he was being shoveled
into a coma. A factory whistle blew.

He numbly paid for his lunch and walked across the street. Joe tagged along and felt the weight of the old man's apathy. It, was like watching a turtle trudge through wet cement.

They stopped in front of the factory's freight entrance, and the old man shut his eyes and shook his head as if he were trying to escape a hangover. He walked to the elevator and Joe sat on a pump in the street and the old man came back and gave Joe a dime and walked back to the elevator, his body slumped and his head still shaking. *I ain't got nobody and nobody cares for me.*

Joe ran across the street and into the lunch wagon and asked for a hot dog, plenty of mustard, plenty of sauerkraut.

The counterman said: The great villain of the American stomach coming up—with apologies to the pigs!

Joe spluttered jubilance as he watched the counterman squirt mustard over the dog and reach for the sauerkraut.

The counterman said: What's wrong with the old man?

Joe said: Aw, my brother's gotta goddamn weak heart!

The counterman said: A weak heart's no joke.

Joe plunged the dog into his mouth. Some of the sauerkraut fell on his pants.

The counterman said: Well, that's the way the world goes, son, some got it, some ain't.

Joe dabbed his tongue over the mustard stuck to his fingers and saw himself through a mirror behind the counter. He was aggravated by the part in his hair. He felt it was a goddamn cargo to unload at once.

He asked the counterman: Hey, Mister, look: howdaya think I'd look in a pompadour?

He wished for a comb.

CHAPTER 19

THE SCREAM of the factory whistle sliced the stillness of the young evening and the elevators slid to the street level and the workers filled the street with their bodies and their talk. The old man headed for the park. *Me and my shadow, not a soul to tell our troubles to.*

He sat on a bench and watched the last fling of the kids on the swings while their mothers were getting ready to go back home and prepare supper for their men. The park suddenly became clear and silent. He got up and walked to the lake. A large plane was shooting in and out of the white clouds.

He fell to the grass by the edge of the lake and saw a butterfly swoop along the grass with the swirling grace of a ballet dancer, and a boy and a girl were wrapped together very tightly in a rowboat in the middle of the lake.

He recalled the hot summer days he spent in rowboats with the pretty girls of East St. Louis and how they'd wrap themselves together very tightly with arms and legs. He pressed his face to a clump of grass. The itch to sleep came easily.

I tell you he's not a bad boy, Henry. He's a wild boy, a wild boy, not a bad boy. And please don't hit him, Henry. Hitting won't get results. And let this be the last time you send him to bed without his supper. The last time, Henry. Please, Henry, for my sake. He's our only one. We must educate our only one, not hit him. Please, Henry.

There's something in Harry I don't like, Phyllis. He's our son, but there's something in him I don't like. I think he's a bully, Phyllis, a bully. He's too strong for his age and he's taking advantage of the boys in his class. Why, he nearly broke the jaw of Mitchell Tane's boy. And Tane's boy is a small boy, a sick boy, sick and small! I don't like bullies, Phyllis, son or no son!

Oh, Henry, I'm so glad you're home. Harry's worrying me so much. His teacher sent me a note. Harry split the slateboard with his fist. His fist, mind you! And why should he want to split slateboards? Oh, Henry, read the note!

Harry, Harry, you're always fighting! Why must you have me pleading and pleading with the neighbors saying that you're a good boy and didn't mean to hurt their boys? And you're really a bad boy, Harry. Such a bad boy! And what, what am I going to do with you, you bad boy?

Phyllis, again that piano is in a different spot! Every damn day in a different spot! Some day I'm going to come home and find it on the roof! And supposing he breaks the legs, then what? Must I tell you the price of pianos today, Phyllis? And why in God's name should he want to move pianos, Phyllis? And where the hell does he get his strength? You're skinny and I'm skinny and why the hell isn't he skinny? Jesus Christ, moving pianos, lifting pianos! Jesus Christ, Phyllis, do you hear, Jesus Christ!

We've got to do something about Harry, Henry. He's made a gymnasium of his bedroom! He spends his entire allowance on those horrid Physical Culture Magazines and makes muscles in front of mirrors! He tears telephone books and now he's given me his mattress saying that a mattress softens a man's back, and from now on he's sleeping on a board, a board hardens a man's back, he says! Sleeping on a board! That's too much for me, Henry!

Phyllis, I've been thinking it over. I've gone through some tall thinking. It seems to me that the love Harry has for his body will surely be recorded as one of the great romances of history.

I know you're ashamed to go to Harry's graduation, Henry.

Sixteen years old and just getting out of Public School! If only he'd admire his books as much as he admires his muscles, why, we'd have a genius on our hands! And once we were so proud of him. We had so much hope for him. And now I'm ashamed of him, Henry. Sixteen years old, the oldest boy to ever graduate Public School 18, his teacher said. Henry, I'm going to cry.

Harry, you oughta go inna ring. You got strength to burn. You're another Stanley Ketchell! Say, Harry, my uncle knows a guy who knows a guy who manages fighters. Why don't you look him up, Harry? Nothing to lose, Harry. You got strength to bum!

That's her, Harry! The one with the big headlights! I saw her the other night at the Amusement park drunk with two Wops. She's smiling at you, Harry! Go on and make her! Show your stuff! You got more onna ball than a Wop! Boy, she's a hot one, 23 skidoo! The way she stands, Harry! Oh, Mamma!

Ladies and Gentlemen, on this platform we have Ulysses L. Sampson, the one and only original Ulysses L. Sampson, the strongest man in the world, including the State of Missouri! Mr. Sampson, ladies and gentlemen, will match his strength against any contender in the audience, man, woman or beast! He will lift any chosen weight and invite you to do likewise! And if accomplished, you will receive the magnificent sum of Twenty Five Good American Dollars, the green lucre of Uncle Sam! Come one, come all! Choose the weight for Ulysses L. Sampson and test your own strength! Who shall be the first to try, ladies and gentlemen? Who shall be the first to pit his strength against the one and only original Ulysses L. Sampson? I see a boy coming to the platform! Give him room, give the brave boy room! What is your name, son? Harry Anderson? Ladies and gentlemen, I give you Harry Anderson, a daring specimen of American Youth! What is your choice weight, son? Ulysses L. Sampson is ready!

Oh, Harry, hold me tighter than that. Yes, break my ribs. Oh, Harry, such strength. Kiss me, Harry. Come on, you can do better than that. Say, Harry, people think you made a fool of Ulysses L. Sampson. And, Harry, wottaya gonna do with the twenty-five dollars? Wanna listen to me and my idea? Well, first we'll see the girlie show at Joe Ryan's. Then we'll go to the beach, Harry. Then we'll drink beer at a place that sells the best beer. Then we'll go somewhere, Harry, somewhere where it's dark and cozy. And then, Harry . . . oh, go on, you can hold me tighter than that, Harry!

Harry, you'd better lay low for awhile. You broke that Wop's nose. All his relatives are searching for you. And Wops carry knives, Harry. They think they still live in Italy. Better hide, Harry. Better hide.

Say, son, will you give me a lift? This wagon of mine is stuck in the mud. If you'll push along with me I'll make it worth your while. Okay, let's try it. Say, you have remarkable strength! Pushed it clear out of the mud! Take this dollar, son! What strength! Man alive!

Harry, you must listen to me. Your mother and I are worried about you. You started high school and you haven't attended one day of class. And you come home drunk every night with that riff-raff from the bridge. Now, Harry, what do you want to do? Do you want to continue school and study something? Or do you want to quit and get a job? One of the two, Harry. It's got to be one of the two. That's final!

Muscles like iron, that's Harry Anderson! Feel his muscle's, one at a time! Get a good feel! Ain't they like iron?

Here's Harry! Harry, this guy'll bet you a dollar you can't bend this pipe. How about it, Harry? Wanna make an easy dollar? There! Hand over that dollar, fella! Gonna have some beer, Harry?

Take it easy with the dames, Harry. Don't burn yourself out at this stage of the game. Sure, they're crazy about you! Who's saying they ain't? But just take it easy. Don't lose your youth on tramps, that's all. Your youth's important. You're a young guy, Harry. Save some of your stuff for a wife and kids.

Hear what Harry did the other day? He picked up a horse and carried it a block, that's what Harry did! Tell them what you did, Harry!

Geez, Harry, alla guys are damn sorry your old lady kicked off. First your old man and now your old lady. A mother's a guy's best friend. That's what the Good Book says, Harry. Geez, wottaya gonna do now, Harry?

The job pays eight dollars a week, my boy. Take it or leave it. Okay, the hours run from eight to eight, a dollar a day, good pay these days. Be on time, work hard, don't watch the clock, keep away from the women, keep away from the booze, learn the business from a to z and you'll get ahead. Remember what I say and I guarantee you a damn decent future. Let's get to work.

Friday,

My strong adorable Harry,

I got to be frank. You said you'd marry me. The other night in bed you said you'd marry me. You said where was I all your life? Harry, I was in Kansas City all your life. Oh, Harry, what's wrong? But I got to be frank. I know what's wrong. Yes, I do. Somebody told me that somebody told you I was a dirty whore. Harry, I ain't a dirty whore. Ask Kansas City people if I'm a dirty whore. My reputation in Kansas City was very clean. I worked in a library there. Whores don't work in libraries, Harry.

Oh, Harry, if I do things with you it ain't because I'm a whore. It's because I love you and love is clean. Harry, please don't listen to lies. Please see the girl who loves you. Please see the girl who wants to be Mrs. Harry Anderson. Please, Harry, I'm no dirty whore and don't ditch me. Last night I was all alone in bed and I missed you like anything and I cried and I cried and, Harry, I think I'll die if you leave me flat.

I love you like nobody's business, sweet Harry, and please break the dirty neck of that dirty somebody who told you I was a dirty whore.

The Girl You Said You'd Marry,

Flo.

P.S. I got to tell you the truth, Harry. I never worked in a library. I didn't mean to lie, Harry. I didn't mean to lie to the adorable man who said he'd marry me the other night in bed.

This is a respectable boarding house, Mr. Anderson. We don't allow drinking in the rooms, cooking in the rooms and, above all, women in the rooms. The rent is four dollars a week. Fresh linen every two weeks. Change of towels every Friday noon. And my boarders pay in advance. Thank you, Mr. Anderson. I'll leave your receipt under your door.

I'm not complaining about your work, Harry, but for Christ's sake, you're always late, late every goddamn morning! And I don't like the color of your eyes. They're red from booze. Take a tip from an old timer, keep away from the stuff. Sorry to let you go, Harry. Damned sorry, do you hear?

Harry, if I hadda dollar wouldn't I give it to you? Wouldn't I,

Harry? Tell the truth, wouldn't I? Hell, you're the best pal a guy ever had! But, Harry, my friend, I ain't gotta dollar! Search me if you don't believe me! Go on, search me! Search the best pal you ever had!

Well, if it ain't Harry Anderson! Where've you been? What's with you? You look shot! Say, here's my card! I'm inna pig-iron business! Look me up! See what I can do for you!

So you're Harry Anderson! Guess you don't remember me! Guess you don't remember the girl you left in that room that merry Christmas morning! Guess you don't remember sneaking out without paying me! Remember me now? Maybe I oughta strip! Maybe your memory'll come back! Why, I oughta crack that face of yours! Merry Christmas, you dirty drunken bum!

Holy cats! Harry, Harry, you look like hell! You look like a dead dog!

You can't be Harry Anderson! No, I don't believe it! You must be the ghost of Harry Anderson! You can't kid me! I've been around!

Harry, think of it! You could've been a champ! Another Stanley Ketchell. All you hadda do was look up my uncle! But that was a long time ago, Harry. You could've been a champ a long time ago. But today even the punks around Ryan's kick your ass in and slap you around. Too bad, Harry. You could've been a champ. Goddamn too bad.

Harry, I gotta job for you if you promise to stay onna wagon. It pays okay and you gotta chance to be okay if you just promise to stay onna wagon. Wottaya say, Harry? Shall we shake on it, Harry? Wottaya say?

I'll take you back on one condition, Mr. Anderson, on the one condition that you promise to pay for the mattress you burned on that drunken spree you had. Yes, I still have your clothes. All right, the rent is now six dollars a week, and the mattress will cost you exactly twenty dollars. And your clothes will be in your room when you occupy it tonight. Thank you, Mr. Anderson, and let us have no more trouble. Please!

Harry, you're going great! The foreman says you're a hard worker and you do alla tough work around here even if you ain't as strong as you usta be, or as strong as some of the guys around here. And, say, Harry, you're looking great! Almost like you usta. Glad you're looking like you look. Damn glad!

Drunk again, Mr. Anderson! I'm sorry, but you'll just have to find yourself another room. And that girl you had in your room last Wednesday night was not your sister, Mr. Anderson. I looked you up, Mr. Anderson. You never had a sister, Mr. Anderson!

Harry, do yourself a favor, a big one. Lay off the stuff. Do it for good this time. No more one week off and one month on. The foreman says you ain't working like you usta. Get wise, Harry. Smarten up. You're not the strong bull of the good old days. Get wise, will you, Harry?

Well, well, well! Harry Anderson inna flesh and blood! Wottaya drinking, Harry? You ain't drinking? Hey, fellas, Harry ain't drinking! Maybe you'd like pop soda, Harry? Gus, you got pop soda for strong guy Harry Anderson? Aw, that's too stinking bad! Sorry, Harry, Gus got no pop soda! I feel awful bad! Oh, I feel so awful bad!

See the new guy, Harry? The big guy with the big head? Punches like a mule, Harry. Rammed his fist clean through a barrel the other day. 'Fraid you wouldn't stand a chance with him, Harry. Not the way you look. No, not the way you look.

The foreman told me to tell you you're fired, Harry. Says he needs strong guys around here. Seems it's a strong guy's world, Harry. See you sometime.

Imagine me, Harry, Danny Feeny, Daniel Q. Feeny, having a place of my own! Well, I have! All my own! My own place, my own boss! And I need a man, Harry. Come around tomorrow. Here's my card. Imagine me, Danny Feeny, having cards? Come around, Harry. See what I can do for you.

Say, what's happened to that Harry Anderson? Remember what a battling boozer he was? Now he's quiet, so quiet and drinks water by the gallon. He works for Danny Feeny. Danny says alla young heels ride him ragged. Danny says it goes on all day and Harry just takes it and goes on with his work. How about that, fellas? Harry Anderson takes it and just goes on with his work!

Harry, meet Sylvia. Sylvia meet Harry. Sylvia's been dying to meet you, Harry. Now, Sylvia, don't you go and blush. You know you've been on pins and needles to meet Harry Anderson. Harry, I tell you she drives Mrs. Feeny deaf, dumb and blind with questions about you. Well, here you are, Sylvia. Here's Harry Anderson in person!

Mr. Anderson, please don't think me bold, but we lived next door to you for years and years and I cried when your mother and father died and went to heaven. I guess you don't remember the little girl with the yellow curls who always sat on the stoop and watched you go to school and come back from school. I guess you don't Mr. Anderson. But I do, Mr. Anderson.

Harry, marry the girl! She's a peach! Pretty as a picture and gotta face like an angel! Cooks a blue streak! Has a helluva sunny disposition! And her shape, Harry! Oh, her shape!

You're not at all too old for me, Harry Anderson! And maybe you're not as strong as you were, but living at home and eating at home and, darling Harry, loving at home will make you as strong as you were. You'll see, Harry. You'll see.

Of course, of course, Harry! You name the day, sweet! I'll tell mother and we'll have a party at our house and mother will ask Father Flaherty to perform the blessings. And, Harry, it will be such a lovely wedding, flowers, cake and all. And I'll be such a good wife, such a good wife, Harry, my beautiful husband.

Mr. Anderson, your wife has just delivered a baby girl, a healthy baby girl! Congratulations, Mr. Anderson!

Harry, don't feel so bad about it not being a boy. Maybe, Harry, maybe the next time. Maybe, Harry, if God is good to us.

We'll call her Mabel, Harry, after my grandmother. Isn't she a darling, Harry? She has your eyes, you know. And, Harry, times are changing and people may change and we must watch over Mabel night and day. Oh, Harry, she's such a darling! Look, she's smiling! Harry, she is smiling! Smile for your Daddy, darling! Harry, she is so smiling!

If it ain't Harry Anderson pushing a baby carriage! Remember when you usta push guys around who thought they were tough? Guess you don't wanna think about that, hey, Harry? Guess you can't afford to think about it when you look like you ain't got the strength to push a carriage. So now you gotta kid. Well, times've changed, all right. Even got one of my own. Name's Bill.

You've been with me for quite awhile, Harry, for quite awhile. And I can say that you gave your strength to the firm. You're my favorite employee. But, Harry, big business don't give a damn for us little guys. They don't care how hard a man works to build a little business to make a little money and be a little happy. Well, Harry, we've been snapped up. Just like that. Snapped up by one of those big money firms. A lot they give a hoot'n hell about how tough my struggle was for ten long years. They own the leather business and I gotta whistle for the goods. So they sunk our ship, Harry. And I'm giving up. I'm selling out. I can't fight big money with little money. I know when I've had enough. Sorry, it came to this, Harry. Give my love to the wife.

It's a boy this time, Harry! I know you wanted a boy! I'm glad it's a boy! Harry, you're smiling! Oh, Harry, I thought you had forgotten how to smile! Is it because of the boy, darling?

Why don't you go to New York, Harry? East St. Louis ain't the place for men who wanna make a living. Especially a man with two kids. Go to New York! See what's what. Heard a lot about the big city and how men get rich and fat. Go on, Harry. Don't waste your life here. And say, Harry, how's little Chesty? Bet he's like a bull! Chip off the old block, right, Harry?

Harry, New York's not like East St. Louis. East St. Louis is a one bed town. New York's a twin bed city. Let us buy twin beds, Harry. Yes, Harry?,

Oh, Harry, I don't think there's no future for you just because your strength is gone. Do you really think so, Harry? Oh, Harry, I don't think so. I think you have brains. I really do think so. And don't think you're old. You're not old at all. And, Harry, do you want me to help you move the parlor chair to the corner of the room? I will if you want me to, Harry.

Harry, I'm afraid of this big city. It's so big, so terribly big. Harry, we must take care of Mabel every single day, every single day, Harry, without fail. We must make it our duty. And Chesty mustn't run around too much. I've heard a lot about these New York boys turning into thieves and murderers, and, excuse me for saying such things, raping the girls and living in jails. And, Harry, I think we're getting one more. If it's a boy, darling, we'll call him Joseph! That was your grandfather's name, wasn't it, Harry?

Imagine meeting you, Harry Anderson in New York, big New York! Well, things ain't just like they usta be, I guess. Once we were kids with tough bodies. Now, well, Harry, guess we're just a couple of old wrecks. Youth must be served. I once read that inna book.

Pop, how many damn times must I move around this damn furniture? One day here, the next day there! And the way you sit around and watch me, just watch me. Pop, tell me, why do you get such a helluva kick out of watching me? Jesus H. Christ!

Harry, you're not looking well. You're getting thinner and thinner. And, Harry, I'm sick, too. I don't know what it is. I get those pains I spoke to you about. They're the craziest pains. Mabel and Chesty are studying. Mabel's such a good girl. I'm combing her hair differently even though she likes it the way she combs it now and cried when I suggested a change. But I know best, Harry. And, oh, you should see the pretty blouse I bought for her! Fancy figures and all! She doesn't like it now, but she'll get used to it. And, Harry, please take the very best care of yourself. And, darling, see how little Joseph is behaving.

Harry, you should have gone to a drugstore! How in the world can we afford one more?

Thank the good Lord you have a steady job, Harry. With times as they are and four mouths to feed I don't know how we'd get along if you didn't have a steady job. And please don't be angry, Harry, but Chesty asked me to tell you to please stop staring at him, and to stop asking him questions if he likes to fight and lift things. I told him you mean no harm, but he asked me to tell you this just the same. And, Harry, Joseph is turning into a terrible ruffian. He has the loudest mouth. God knows where he picks up that language! I was shocked when he called the baby Skinny! Skinny, mind you, Harry!

Chesty, I must talk to you. I know you like school, and I know you're a good student, but you'll just have to leave school. And it breaks my heart to ask you to do it, but your father is making so little and living is so hard and food is so high and rent is so high and it breaks my heart to ask you to leave school when you're such a good student. I hate myself for asking you to do it.

Harry, Mabel yelled at me today. We had a terrible fight. And after all I've done for her. She just turned on me and screamed. It was simply because I opened the bathroom door and found her running her hands over her naked breasts before a mirror. Her naked breasts, Harry! I told her it was a sin. And she screamed that from here on I should knock when a door is closed. And the way she screamed! Good God in heaven, Harry, the way she screamed!

I like books, Pop. I like the guys who write the books, and

sometimes I can't stand the guys who write the books. But don't waste your time telling me I'm wasting my time reading books, Pop. It just won't do you any good. No damn good. I think you get the general idea, Pop.

Mabel's becoming unbearable, Harry. She absolutely refuses to do anything I ask her to do. Harry, you talk to her. Tell her to obey me. Oh, Harry, tell her to obey me!

Look, Pop, look. I don't want to work on a truck. I don't want to work on a dock. The American Railway Express doesn't interest me. I want to get into something where I can use my head, my head. I get a kick out of using my head! Where the hell is the beauty of using your muscles for a living? Have a heart, Pop!

The War!

Chesty, father's friend, Bert Adams, says that the Johnson Motor Company needs young men for defense work. Now, Chesty, please do it for my sake. You've been searching for your kind of work long enough. I know you may get that job with the publishing company, but Bert said you can make lots more money in defense work, and he said that you should ask for a Mr. Bibs Malkind, he's in the main office. And, Chesty, please give this sort of work a chance for my sake. You'll make me happy and you'll make father happy, too. And listen to your mother, Chesty, and you too will be happy. Won't he, Harry? Tell him he will, Harry.

The telegram read: YOU HAVE BEEN SELECTED FOR APPOINTMENT IN THE WAR DEPARTMENT AS CAF 2 CLERK. REPORT FOR DUTY APRIL 21ST AT 8.30 TO CIVILIAN PERSONNEL, BUILDING H AT 22ND AND C STREET, WASHINGTON, D. C.

Mother, I'm going to Washington! Now, mother, don't put on any acts! I don't care what you say! I don't care what you say! Do you hear, mother? I don't care what you say. I'm going to Washington and that's that! Oh, your pain, my eye!

Harry, I miss our little girl. I'm worried about her. I haven't slept a wink in weeks. And, Harry, talk to Joe. Tell him not to pick on our poor little one. Oh, Harry, I'm so worried about Mabel.

They gave Chesty a raise, Harry. He said that they said he was dependable. But he's not happy. He's not happy at the Johnson Motor Company even though they gave him a raise. Why, Harry?

Harry, do you think we should buy a bed for Chesty now that there's a little money in the house? Or should we wait until the war is over. I hate to think of our three boys in one bed. Don't you, Harry?

Well, this is a Greeting from the President, Pop. I'm in 1A and I must report for my physical induction. Looks like I'm being picked to save the world from fascism, Pop.

Harry, I must go to Washington. Not one letter from Mabel in such a long time. And there's been so many rapes there! What if poor little Mabel . , , oh, Harry, I must go at once! Take care of the children, Harry. Take good care of them. And take care of yourself, Harry. I'll be back soon.

Nothing to eat in this goddamn house! No nothing! No god-damn nothing! Hey, Pop, how about some money for me and Skinny to go out and eat? How about it, Pop? How about some god-damn money?

Western Union for Mr. Harry Anderson! You, Mr. Harry Anderson? Sign here, Mr. Anderson. Telegram from Washington. Thanks, Mr. Anderson. . . . MAMMA DEAD. BE HOME TOMORROW, WILL EXPLAIN. . . . MABEL.

You think I can lift a piano, Pop? . . . Do me a favor and change your brand of cigarets.

What a house! . . . I'm in no mood to grow old over a stove! . . . Find a wife! . . . Don't waste your life in a cold bed!

Is that your manifesto?

Madame Zavette reads your life, past, present and future. She never fails to reunite the separated . . . her advice will overcome enemies and bad luck of all kinds. . . . Consult the Madame . . . $2.

Pop, how's your woman? . . . You're a poet, Pop. . . . I wouldn't be found dead with Sam Duncan! . . . Where do you get off working in a steel mill, you old bum? . . . Jump inna river! Drown yourself! . . . You're stinking up the joint! . . . Screw, bum! . . . See where I kicked him? Right inna spine!

Leave the poor old man alone!
Leave the poor old man alone!
Leave the poor old man alone!

Spare a dime, Mister? Need some coffee in my belly. . . . You're a buddy, Mister.

In the mood for the time of your life, Mister? . . . I'm good for what ails you, Mister.

Pop, I gotta talk to you! . . . Listen, Pop, are you listening? . . . Pop, the Army don't want Chesty!

Pop, the Army don't want Chesty!

Pop, the Army don't want Chesty!

Pop, the Army don't want Chesty!

CHAPTER 20

THE OLD man awoke in a paralytic fright, trembling and wet from the grass, and his hands were clenched in red and white palms. A mosquito nipped his leg, and two men were trotting down the road. A boy was calling a girl's name.

The shine of the low moon made the lake look like a rich spread of shiny ink, and the desolate pitch of the black night and the dead vacuum of the empty lake made him feel dwarfed and puny, and desperate. He knew that he felt this way many times before, so closely versed with his misshapen life and its scattered remnants, and he knew that Chesty was his final humiliation, and he knew how hard he tried to beg him, argue with him, reason with him, woo him, how he tried to groom him to be what he, Harry Anderson, wanted to be, strong and proud, respected and feared. Chesty was to be his reason for continuing life, his replacement, his salvation. And now Chesty had failed him. And now Chesty was reduced to the low peg of physical poverty, a sick cat in a cellar. Chesty was no more his lone hope of leaving a niche in the shafts of the minds of the multiple people who violated him and slandered him with the stinging truths he knew and didn't want to know. Chesty was no more his contribution to himself, his survival. *Chesty, Chesty, Chesty!* Father and son, outstanding members of the Lost Battalion.

Nobody knows the trouble I've seen.

He felt the cruel effect of plodding across his last stage, the third act, cheated of an honorable glory, a feeble shell waiting for the black curtain to fall over an epileptic stage, a barren system of skinny flesh kept intact by a slight trickle of blood . . . and now the epilogue.

A swift rage blew up in his bony body. He was able to feel it spurt and sense its flow. And Chesty's face grew fleshy before him, and the face was the last straw on his back, and he ached to spoil the face and soil the texture and have him realize the constant scar of misery his father was enduring every day and night in the shapeless sanctuary he had erected through the years.

Oh, how he once toyed with the magnificent unity of Harry and Chesty Anderson living together, loving together, fighting together, hating together and laughing together and drinking together and walking the streets together searching and never stop searching for trouble and excitement, trouble and excitement and more trouble and excitement. Never stop searching!

Harry and Chesty Anderson, knitted into one fabric!

Harry and Chesty Anderson, two in one!

Harry and Chesty Anderson!

Harry and Chesty!

The Anderson Boys!

Oh, but that was long ago!

All the world is sad and dreary everywhere I roam.

His wounds were open for infection.

He headed for home in the world he tried to make.

CHAPTER 21

Look down, look down that lonesome road before you travel on.

He saw the outline of his house in the dimout. *All his life he lived in a house, a house, always a house, never a home.* He yearned to make a dash for it, but his legs were too old to permit such an opulent license. He struck the happy medium of walking briskly, and he was unable to control the dribbling jag of his fists. He stuck them deep in his pockets and they wouldn't lie still. He pacified them by letting them hang by his sides.

He stepped on a dead cigar in the gutter, and the sensitive symbol of a dead cigar in a gutter generated a continuity of spleen, and his fists became berserk. He fastened his fingers more tightly into his palms and he watched his fists as the house he lived in grew visible in the dark and he was reminded of two tight hunks of ham. He walked up the steps, two at a time. His rage sprang crazily.

He opened the door of his sons' bedroom and saw the sleeping, naked bodies of his three sons, and the body of Chesty, sprawled in the white of the bed brought his rage to its meridian. *Let the punishment fit the crime.*

He lifted his fists high and brought them down on Chesty's face, and he lifted them again and again and hammered and hammered the body and the face, the body, the face, the body, the face, the body, the face, and Chesty's eyes were open, and he saw the old man's fists in the air and felt the rain and the turgid pain of the blows hammering his body and face, and the echo of a scream choked all the organs of his body, and he thought of his heart, and he wanted to cry out loudly about his heart. *Now, Chesty, don't get excited. Tell you what, Chesty: have some tea, milk, crackers, a pill, a couple of pills, but don't get excited, don't get excited, no, no, not that, not that.*

But the helpless terror and the bewildered terror smothered the cry, and he looked at his brothers and their eyes were open to witness his terror and the old man's fists, and he saw the tears in Skinny's eyes, and he wanted to hold him very close and tell him how he felt so very close to him, and he looked at Joe and Joe was grinning and glowing, and he looked up at the old man and saw the face of an old beast, and he was captured by some hungry appetite to inspect the livid welts that coughed from his body and face, but the drive of the saturating fists drained his senses, and he collapsed into an endless pit of exhaustion, and the room became a frenzied whirlpool, and he was being sucked into the whirlpool, and everything went around and down like a ball rolling around and down and down a hill, down, down, around and down, the ball rolled and rolled down, down, around and down and down the hill, and the pain in his body stopped screaming, and the canopy of the soaking blows that came like the precise rhythm of a fugue were incapable of penetrating the blankness, the catacombs of his mind. No, not any more.

I TALK WITH ALAN KAPELNER
Seymour Krim

(This interview originally appeared in Seymour Krim's 1970 collection of essays, *Shake It for the World, Smartass*. It has been reproduced here with permission from the author's estate.)

Kapelner (too little known) is seasoned, unique, resourceful, beautifully cocky toward existence and humble to individuals he respects, a writer lying in wait for readers, practically undiscovered in the overpopulated wilderness of the U.S. 60s.

KRIM: . . . I want to get to what you mean when you say you want your literary men to make statements? Do you mean direct statements, or do you mean symbolic statements, or—

KAPELNER: Well, statements in terms of one's time, saying something about the world you live in, whether it's in terms of love or hate, or pity, or complete venom. I think that Camus made a powerful statement in *The Stranger* and in *The Plague*. I think one of the most powerful statements Sartre has made has been in *Nausea*. I don't think he realized it, and maybe that's why it wasn't so "fixed" in terms of his other work. This is what I call a statement. The *Underground Notes* of Dostoevsky; Raskolnikov as an individual is an immense statement for the fellows of his time. See, what I think is wrong in writing today is that everyone writes as if sex is it, sex is everything. And . . . that everything is in a room. It's a girl and a guy in a room; a man and a wife in a room. Well, I don't look upon this as a statement. I think this is a very personal way of writing. Some of the work is excellent, but I personally can't go beyond the excellence.

KRIM: What was the statement you were making or trying to make in your first book, *Lonely Boy Blues?*

KAPELNER: Well, in short, and possibly also in essence, it's just the failed men and women, greedy, hungering to resurrect themselves in their children. To relive their lives in their children, never realizing they're destroying their children. Now this is all over the world today, and this is why we have the children saying the elders are terrible, bad, no goddamn good, they stink. I'm convinced this is what I was attempting to say in *Lonely Boy Blues.*

KRIM: What was the statement you were after in *All the Naked Heroes?*

KAPELNER: That's a very difficult thing. See, in *All the Naked Heroes* I wasn't too certain. *Heroes* was improvised from beginning to end. I didn't know what was coming next. Two brothers, one with the total inability to face a crisis, another brother with the ability to go beyond the crisis on the basis of possibly the crisis doing him a hell of a lot of good. I'm not too sure, as the guy who wrote the book, if that is a statement as I previously tried to describe it.

KRIM: I'm getting to a problem that I want to pursue. You said, and I agree with you, that the literary art that is most interesting is that which makes a statement. At the same time, you also know the dangers—we saw them in the Marxist 30s over here—of propagandistic art which is all statement and no art.

KAPELNER: Yeah, but those fellows were hired men. They were hired not on a basis of financially being paid, they were hired on a basis of being tied to a locomotive. You know Lenin said, "The locomotive of history." They were passengers on that train. There was no stopping for them. Someone once said, maybe it was Koestler, that they were Artists in Uniform. Well, that's what they were. I'm without uniform. I am with uniform, my own uniform, but those fellows of that period, the women of that period, were very idealistic. I never went along with the idealism.

KRIM: Alan, I want to cut into your thoughts and approach the problem from a different direction. You said earlier that what you want in a writer is a statement, finally.

KAPELNER: Not what I want in a writer, what I'd like to see in a writer.

KRIM: I get the distinction and acknowledge it. Do you think that writers who become too hipped on making statements lose some of the subtlety of their art?

KAPELNER: No, not if the writer is a good man and has eyes, ears, a feeling for sound, smell. I don't see why he should. I think we're getting hung up on the word "statement." Maybe it should be put in terms of a man speaking to his time. That doesn't mean he'd be hung up on anything. I think he's a free man once he gets that way, providing that no one is impinging upon his emotions, no outfit of any kind, no hip group or political group. Does that sound right?

KRIM: Yes. But let me go back. Because when I asked you specifically about your own books you honestly said that you didn't know if they contained the kind of statement—

KAPELNER: Well, I think that *Lonely Boy Blues* contains a statement. By God, I believe it contains a very big statement. It was only years later that fellows like Dan Wakefield said, "Gee, you did it so long ago, and now people are getting on that sort of thing without even knowing of *Lonely Boy Blues.*" *All the Naked Heroes* was a pile-up, a conglomeration that piled up into moods, emotions, which made for a kind of a pyramid. Now whether it's a statement as I see it, I can't be too sure. I may have failed because of the looseness of the improvisation.

KRIM: Every writer improvises, it seems to me, even just to find the imagery for his statement. If you're a novelist or a dramatist, you do it with people and scenes and characters, and so on, and you usually don't know the precise arrangements your mind is going to make during the act of writing, isn't that correct?

KAPELNER: Yes.

KRIM: But yet you seemed to say before, a little wistfully, that you were improvising and you improvised yourself away from your statement.

KAPELNER: No, I didn't mean it that way at all. I think we are getting stuck with that specific word "statement." You know, it just occurred to me that the marvelous writers who were of their time and saying something to their time and if possible going beyond their time, were the political and social animals and the sexual animals, I think of these three elements, politics, sociality, sex. You see, when you go back and look at people, say, from the Greeks on, you'll always find the best men were very political and very social. They were political animals, social animals, and God knows we have very few of them when you think of the great mass of writers, and just the few who had that quality.

KRIM: Let me ask you this: I know that your inclinations among presentday writers run to men like Malraux, Camus, Sartre. Now how do you deal with a man like Céline, who was a rightist and who I'm sure you'll admit was a brilliant writer, but was outside of your tradition of the explicit political and social animal?

KAPELNER: Céline, like Genet, like Burroughs, like a few others I can't recall at the moment, and even in a sense like Oscar Wilde, I don't know if these men are important to their time. I always looked upon them as the exotic flowers of literature. Céline I think is a very fair example. Genet is an excellent example of this. I can't for the life of me find them uninteresting. But I can't put them alongside of men involved, *committed*, I think that could be the word more than a "statement," committed to their time.

KRIM: What makes you say that Camus or Malraux are more committed to their time than Céline or Genet?

KAPELNER: I am only basing what I say on their work. You see, Genet is more interested in the homosexual apparatus, and on that basis alone he's an exotic flower; and Burroughs' interest is in the hung-up scene, the dope scene, whatever the scene might be, but all based on the needs of either enthusiasm or retreat. These are the exotics. They're not speaking to a time at large. They're speaking to a certain sector of people, they are obviously very significant to these people, and sometimes quite significant to me.

KRIM: In other words, if I can translate this into my own terms, you think that they're too private in their preoccupations.

KAPELNER: And also precious.

KRIM: Don't you think the soil of the contemporary world is conducive to that kind of work? More so perhaps than ever before?

KAPELNER: Yes, but this doesn't put them in the state of largeness. They're so narrow, they're confined, they're working from within their own cells. They're cell-addicted, cell-oriented, and the others are not—they're walkers, talkers, they move around. Genet doesn't move around. Burroughs doesn't move around. Céline never moved around. Of course, being a Jew, I dislike Céline on other levels.

KRIM: Proust, you'll admit, was a large writer, and yet he worked out of a specialized "cell" as well.

KAPELNER: Well—and this might sound awfully precious, possibly—if a man sings, if he's a singer, like Joyce was a singer, and he's a composite, or he contains, or he's an eater, a devourer of sights, scenes, smells, and it pours out of him like a crazy, weird, but yet very super-real song, he is not going to be confined, he is not going to be in a cell, in short he's a free man, 'cause he's singing all that. The others are not free, those you've named. Proust is a special case entirely. Right now I can't put my finger on why I think he's—I *know*—he's a special case. But he's a far superior man than the Burroughses and the Célines and the Genets. Proust has a certain kind of power, a neurotic, lonely power, you know. There's something very sickly about Proust. But he's a very, very special sort of case.

KRIM: You say, and you mean it, that you want your writer or artist to be a free man. And yet think back on the men who have made the biggest marks on literature. Most of them were neurotics or compulsives, even those who stood for freedom were "sick" compared to the majority.

KAPELNER: Neuroses and psychoses have nothing to do with freeness. A man could be free and be psychotic or neurotic and so I don't understand that point you make.

KRIM: Let me say it again.

KAPELNER: Let me say something right now. Maybe this is it . . . freeness in the terms that he has made his own philosophy, his own psychology, his own feelings, his own song, or even his own lack of song. That he is not an annex to any main chancellery or main corridor of society. That he's his own man. In that, I think a man is free.

KRIM: In other words, you're asking for originality?

KAPELNER: Yes, yes. I think one of the great troubles today is that literature has gone into a Hollywood syndrome. And even the so-called good writers have gone into this syndrome. They're writing the same song, the same scene, the same chazarei. The same junk.

KRIM: Alan, your first book *Lonely Boy Blues* came out in what year?

KAPELNER: 45

KRIM: 1945. Your next novel came out in—

KAPELNER: 60.

KRIM: What took up those 15 years?

KAPELNER: Well, after *Blues* I didn't know what to do with my time. I screwed around a lot, I wasted a lot of years. I knew I wanted to go on writing . . . But I just never got to it. I look back at it, and retrospection is not, of course, always true, it's always a little manufactured. I suppose I wanted to live, you know. Now that's a terrible cliché, but it also is an excellent truth. I wanted to live, I wanted to see, I wanted to get around. I first came down to the Village then, I didn't know what life was like, I wanted to see paintings.

KRIM: You wrote *Lonely Boy* before you came to the Village.

KAPELNER: Yeah.

KRIM: How long did *All The Naked Heroes* take in the writing, all told?

KAPELNER: Seven years.

KRIM: I see. So a good part of that 15 years went into the *Naked Heroes?*

KAPELNER: Well, I wrote that book and I originally called it *Strangers in the Midnight World*, and a lot of publishers told me to put it away. It was during the McCarthy period. Random House and a few others, there were letters from them asking me to put it away, someone up at Little, Brown, put it away, they wanted to give me money for another novel. I found it very difficult to put away. I got quite a lot of letters, and always specifically, "This is not the time for a book of this kind." Well, then I read the book and I said, I don't understand these people, why shouldn't it be a book for any time, you know, but of course there were people in states of fear. You know what McCarthy did to them. I've always felt that McCarthy was never a villain anyway, it's the people who were in fear of him who were the villains. McCarthy was just some Irish square from Wisconsin, and people just fell by the wayside, fled their attitudes, fled their brains, fled their courage, and made a monster of a man. But the true monsters were those who were the makers of the monster.

KRIM: Yes. But let's not get sidetracked by McCarthy.

KAPELNER: So I read the book. I went up in the country and spent the whole summer reading that book and I said it's a lousy book. I thought I'd write this entire book over again from beginning to end. And that took me quite a long time because I invested a great deal in this book. And I got used to a sense of language which never occurred to me before. Certain sounds of words, rhythms, feelings for words. It could be one of the debits of *All the Naked Heroes*, the romance with words. So then I finished it, McCarthy was gone, and I had no trouble getting it published.

KRIM: How have the critics received your two novels?

KAPELNER: Oh, exceptionally. Strangely enough. The people out West saw more in the work than the people of the East, and that could be because of the sense of jadedness in the East, which is plausible, because the people of the East are more afflicted by the mass media than the people of the West. There's a little more of an openness about them, the ability to receive. The tendency of the people of the East is that jaded feeling, "Aw now, come on man, what the hell is this all about," you know, they are the beneficiaries of such shit that keeps coming, that shit becomes a habit with them.

KRIM: How did the books sell?

KAPELNER: Not well.

KRIM: Both went into paper?

KAPELNER: Both went into paperback. They were published in Holland, England, and Germany. One was a book club selection. *All the Naked Heroes.* Book Find Club. Didn't sell too well. The publisher did have a strong belief that *All the Naked Heroes* would sell very very well. Unfortunately, he was wrong. As far as *Lonely Boy Blues* was concerned, the editor was Maxwell Perkins. Perkins never believed the book would sell, but he believed that the man who wrote the book would be honored.

KRIM: You mean critically honored?

KAPELNER: Critically honored. He thought that was very important.

KRIM: So he was vindicated.

KAPELNER: He was right. I have always felt that more than three-quarters of Max Perkins' attitudes and feelings and beliefs were always right anyway.

KRIM: In your opinion, is this "blind" instinct what made him a great editor?

KAPELNER: Yes. Because he had no planned design in him at all. He could read any kind of literature and he had a very beautifully instinctive touch, very deep. I don't understand some of the people I met later on, people of the *Partisan Review* crowd and the *Com-*

mentary people, who looked upon him as a square. Well, all I can say is I wish they would be as square as he.

KRIM: Alan, about this question of money, and sales. We live in a money culture. You're a rebel in the money culture as a writer. Is there not a kind of poetic or prosetic justice to the fact that your books have had modest sales?

KAPELNER: Would you clear that up a bit?

KRIM: Is it appropriate that the books have had small sales because of their point of view? What makes a book sell a lot of copies anyway?

KAPELNER: I don't know. I think every book is a gamble. Very few publishers will pick a book in terms of prestige. The days of Horace Liveright, as the oldtimers say, that's gone. If they believe it'll sell, they do take a gamble. In many cases it's a dishonorable gamble because they're gambling with something they don't believe in to begin with. Now as far as my work is concerned . . . let me put it this way. It was absolutely shocking to me when the publisher of *All the Naked Heroes* said to me he thought we were going to make a lot of money on that book.

KRIM: That's what I wanted to ask you. When you write a book, you certainly don't write it to sell a lot of copies?

KAPELNER: I hope I would sell a lot of copies. My God, I'd like to make a million dollars on a book! It's on my terms, I'm not prostituting myself. The point is, I'm writing it for people, people buy books. According to the contract I get a certain percentage. The more people who buy books the more people who read what I have to say to them. I'm not a closet writer; I have a big craving in me. The craving is to say what I want to say, how I want to say it, and hope a hell of a lot of people will read it.

KRIM: Alan, you once used the expression that in order to do justice to someone like Céline you really had to "struggle to be objective." I thought it was a good phrase. Try to struggle to be objective now at this question that I'd like to ask you. Some writers, and we've run into them, we discussed Dahlberg just the other day over coffee, become bitter with the years because they don't feel they've gotten the recognition they deserved. It's likely that you feel that some of your contemporaries have gotten more acclaim or have sold more books or perhaps even more important, the so-called serious critics have devoted more pages to their work than to your own. Perhaps. How do you balance all these things within yourself?

KAPELNER: Why, I suppose it would be based on my own makeup that I can't allow the luxury of despair.

KRIM: You mean this as a man or as a writer?

KAPELNER: As a writer and a man. I also can't allow anyone's "victory" being my defeat, and I've always felt this way. My whole feeling, you know, every writer, every guy, every woman who wants to write or paint or dance, I don't care what they want to do, they're in their own boat and they're going to go to their own shores. I know when I get to be 50, 60, 70, I'm not going to vegetate like a lot of oldtimers that cry in some sort of a wild asylum they've built around themselves, and get Jehovah-addicted, you know, "Why have the gods forsaken me?" I was never able to do that. I was a ballplayer. There were better ballplayers than I. I could never feel any envy or jealousy if someone hit a double and I got up and struck out. In a high-school basketball game, if I shot 15 points and someone on my team had 30 points, you know, I could never possibly envy him 'cause I was glad the team won.

KRIM: So you're saying that thankfully you lack some of these competitive streaks?

KAPELNER: No, that isn't it. You know Martha Graham said a very marvelous thing. She said, whether she actually believes it or not, and I'm always a little suspicious about people who write certain things, she said that she's not in competition with anyone, she's only in competition with herself, to better herself. And then when she betters herself she sees her other limitations and she tries to override them. Well, I was very struck by that when I read it about 10 years ago. To the point of cutting it out of the newspaper or magazine, wherever I read it, and sticking it above my desk.

KRIM: I assume that this is your way of answering my question. What do you foresee for yourself in the future?

KAPELNER: Well, I'm not going to go to my grave with a shelf of books, that's a cinch.

KRIM: It's too fucking hard to write one good one?

KAPELNER: Of course. I think if you make it on one book, that's enough. You know. I mean, you've had it.

KRIM: You really think that?

KAPELNER: Yeah, if you make a great message. And I'm not talking about Communist Party messages, or Norman Thomas messages, or that sort of stuff, but I mean your own personal message. And if you've made it strong, and you've made it violent and sweet, just what this whole society, this whole world is like, that's a pretty good thing to have done.

KRIM: All right, you've done it twice, or at least you've—

KAPELNER: I don't think for a moment that I've really written what I have in me.

KRIM: Then there probably will be a few more books, there have to be?

KAPELNER: Yeah. See, I'm never going to be senile, 'cause I've made up my mind never to be senile. So I'm gonna write a—I don't know how many books I'll write but I'm not going to reach a state where I'll be unable to write a book. Because I've seen too many old men who have made it strong and well at one time. And then they get to be about 60, 70 and they have fallen into their own private soft cells. And they're tired, and they're no longer hungry. I think my nature will never allow me to be filled.

KRIM: Do you have any notions as to what your next project is going to be?

KAPELNER: I'd like to write about madness. What I'd like to write is what I think is going to happen in the 70s. The people who are in their 20s now—because they're in complete retreat, they're into the defensive or rather the aggressive mechanism of thinking they're in rebellion. But they're truly in retreat, and then in 10 years, in the 70s, they're going to be in their 30s, and they're gonna be old men with nothing. And I think you're going to see a lot of madness.

KRIM: I'm glad you have a strong theme for another book. How long had you brooded about the massmurder theme of the new book, *The Air-Conditioned Hell?*

KAPELNER: Well, it actually happened on 10th Street and Bleeker one summer night several years ago. And it struck me, the entire thing, of someone—they never did find the killer—but someone, upon reading my book will probably pound on my door, detectives, and say that I've done the killing.

KRIM: Yes, you do feel guilty.

KAPELNER: It's a very intimate book. Maybe I did do the killing, I can't recall. And you know someone said, in dreams we are the greatest of all murderers. Then I did some research on it and I found out there were so many mass-murders. Then there were the individual murders. All this murdering, all this maiming of people. If not a murder, a traumatic maiming. And I saw this whole goddamned society in sort of an alive mausoleum. You know, everyone waiting for death, waiting to be maimed, crippled, hurt, and there was this terrible meanness going around. And meanness coming from the most logical of all reasons, the need for excitement, to escape boredom, monotony, the humdrumness of their time. And that related to Negroes, Puerto Ricans, and Jews, Italians, Wasps, and everyone else. It didn't make a particle of difference. And mind you, I thought of this a hell of a lot, there was nothing improvised about the thinking of this, 'cause I had all the facts before me. And out of it came the idea for the novel. Of a man committing this murder, a mass-murder. Now, I am a slow writer, but it didn't take me long to write this book.

KRIM: I think about two and a half years?

KAPELNER: Yeah. I felt like Jesse Owens writing this book. It was just fantastic, you know. And I first wrote it in first person, I read it and realized I'm not a first person writer. I haven't that knack in the first person. Then I wrote it in third person and it satisfied me.* And that's what this book is all about: a man in revolt against his time, and wanting a better time. And he murders for the better time. See, you had once said in an article that someone's writing was as tough as a murderer. Well, that's what I wanted someone to be, as tough as a murderer, but *commit the act*, so he's beyond being as tough as a murderer 'cause he's now a tough murderer. This story comes from a composite, an avalanche of many similar themes that have happened since World War II ended. There've been so many of these things. Knifers, every damned thing that's been going on. It could be the murder of one, the murder of four or five. Mine was eight.

KRIM: How does a book grow in you? What is the actual process?

KAPELNER: Just sit down and write. Hemingway once said, I believe it was in a letter to Max Perkins, that it took him a long time to find the "habit of writing." I developed the habit of writing. Getting up early in the morning, taking a necessary walk because I knew I'd be sitting all day, and getting back at nine in the morning and having some coffee and just sitting down and writing and sweating it out. My whole writing is always sweating it out.

KRIM: I want to get to a problem that's bigger than both of us. Why is it that when we get down to the typewriter I too sweat it out?

KAPELNER: Because then you have an affair with destiny. Now that sounds terrible, doesn't it? But you do have an affair with destiny.

---

*When this interview was first published in 1970, Kapelner was rewriting his book for yet a third time.

KRIM: You mean the stakes are greater once you put it on a piece of paper?

KAPELNER: Maybe they shouldn't be, but they are. Like you take a prize fighter, you know. You meet him on a street and you spar with him, and he has all the combination punches, and everything, and he bobs and weaves and he smiles, but then you get him in a ring and you wonder, what happened to you, Joe? You were marvelous in the street. But he had no opposition. Once you sit down and write, you have an opposition. Your reader is your opposition. And you have an obligation to yourself, which you don't have when you sit around and talk. Because if I sit around and talk with you, like Seymour we're sitting around, and then you don't agree with me. Oh, all right, man, you don't agree with me, that's perfectly all right. But when I write, Christ, I want you to agree with me. And if you don't, if you don't agree with me—

KRIM: You hate my guts.

KAPELNER: It's not that, I don't hate your guts, but I could blush, you know. I'm not beyond blushing, and that's probably one of my greatest weapons.

1967

ACKNOWLEDGMENTS

Profound thanks are extended to the following individuals for their generous financial support which helped to defray some of this book's production costs:

Kevin Adams, E.R. Auld, Thomas Young Barmore, Jr., Cameron Bennett, Corey Black 101, Brian R. Boisvert, Ian Braddy, Matt Bucher, Jason Burchfield, Brian P. Bullock, Tobias Carroll, Mike Cassella, Stanley Chau, Scott Chiddister, C. Colla, Michael Corkery, Stephen J. Crowley, Jessica DeMarco-Jacobson, Steve Denyer, R. Eggleton, Isaac Ehrlich, Maggie Evans, Pops Feibel, John Feins, Alex J. Funk, Nathan "N.R." Gaddis, GMarkC, Natalie Grand, Rebecca Gransden, Elizabeth Grant, Don Handfield, Mark Hartman, Richard L. Haas III, Erik Hemming, Erik T. Johnson, Brian C. Jones, Handsome Ryan Kennedy, Kurt J. Klemm, Jesse Knepper, James Lamplugh, Chaz Larson, Steve Loiaconi, Frank Loose, Fester L.D. MacKrell, Josh Mahler, Jim McElroy, Brendan McGrath, Doug Milam, Mark S. Mitchell, Steven Moore, Gregory Moses, Geoffrey Moses, David Noller, Michael O'Shaughnessy, @p3rf3kt, Marshall W. Parks, Ry Pickard, Poems-For-All, Matthew J. Rogers, Frank V. Saltarelli, Scarlet, Suzanne Scherrer, Spike Schwab, Connor Shirley, David Starner, Tango Tango, Andrew Tovar, Paul & Laura Trinies, Cato Vandrare, Dan Webb, Jeffrey H. Weinberg - Water Row Books, and Anonymous

Rick Schober
Publisher
Tough Poets Press